The Revenge Seeker

A Sequel to "Goodnight, My Angel"

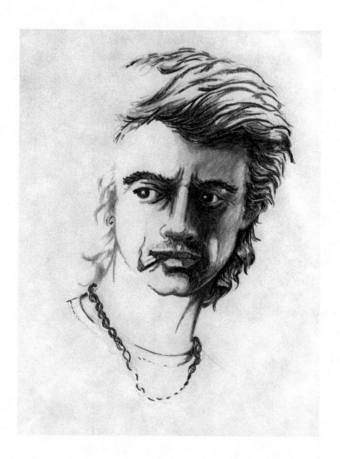

Diane Pellicciotti Kone

authorHOUSE®

AuthorHouse™
1663 Liberty Drive
Bloomington, IN 47403
www.authorhouse.com
Phone: 1-800-839-8640

This is an entirely fictional work, based on certain events in the author's life. All individuals and organizations in the work are solely the author's creation and any resemblance to actual persons, living or dead is coincidental.

First published by AuthorHouse 12/4/2009

ISBN: 978-1-4490-4500-5 (e)
ISBN: 978-1-4490-4498-5 (sc)
ISBN: 978-1-4490-4499-2 (hc)

Library of Congress Control Number: 2009911712

Printed in the United States of America
Bloomington, Indiana

This book is printed on acid-free paper.

Contents

With Heartfelt Appreciation,

I wish to thank my amazing mother, Mary Latini Pellicciotti for her unconditional love and my soul mate and husband, David Kone for his steady support. I am very grateful to my talented and creative uncle, Gino Latini (the sole surviving member of the last generation of Latini brothers) for his cover illustration.

I could not have continued to write without the unswerving encouragement from my friends at Ta Ga Soke. I am also indebted to my grandchildren, Mya, Alea and Makenna Marie Phanhthalath, Robert, Samantha and Alexis Shea, and Kianna, Lauren and Dana Jedrysik for their ability to keep me positive and cheerful. Makenna Marie's valiant strides in overcoming obstacles have been a driving force in my life.

I am also appreciative for all of the initial endorsement from my brother, Joseph Pellicciotti, who read the manuscript in its skeletal form.

Deepest gratitude goes out to my deceased father, Michael Pellicciotti and his brothers and sisters; John Pellicciotti, Dazalene Oaks, Philomena Pyhtila, Carmen Pellicciotti, Lena McLyman and Rose Thomas for teaching me how to "live well" and on the maternal Latini side; those who have gone before me; Dr. Ferdinand Latini, John Latini, Ezio M. Latini, Eleanor Jolley and Anne Struble for teaching me how to "love well." And, to Gertrude Sherman, who came into my life briefly like a shining star, full of beauty and light, I send off to heaven my most sincere "thank you."

I am forever indebted to my beloved Paula for her eternal and everlasting love. She is forever my inspiration.

The Author's Notes

In August of 1981, I gave birth to a very special child. I was ecstatic, totally overjoyed with this tiny wisp of a little human being. My elation was short lived. Soon after her birth, it became evident to the medical staff in attendance that my precious baby was suffering from a rare and serious cardiac defect.

Under the care of excellent physicians, she did well for several years. Sadly, her condition worsened in her preteen years. After suffering severe heart failure and acute cardiac arrest, she became New York State's number one patient on the donor recipient list for a new heart. No heart was available and she passed away. I was worn to shreds by grief. The pain that came from the loss of the beautiful Paula left me shattered. I decided to write her memoirs as a therapy for my wounded soul.

Struggling to find the right words, I embraced the calming quietude and peacefulness of the water's edge to pen my memories of her. Shortly after Paula's untimely death in the spring of 1994, I traveled alone to a small rustic fishing cottage on the St. Lawrence River. My heart was breaking. Looking for a source of peace and closure, I found that writing was curative in helping me to come to terms with the dreadful pain that had overtaken me.

I was on my way to putting my wounded heart back together. The progression was therapeutic. While attempting to heal, the memoirs of the tragedies and treasures of Paula's life were transformed into a manuscript. The manuscript progressed into a book. The book evolved into a romance novel. The romance novel was published and an author was created. The writing bug took hold and would not release itself. I decided to write a sequel to Goodnight, My Angel. Alas, we have The Revenge Seeker!

Diane P. Kone

"The Revenge Seeker"
is lovingly dedicated in the memory of my beloved daughter,

Paula Mary Daniels
"So sweet, too young, too soon"

August 15, 1981 to May 9, 1994

When I must leave you
for a little while
Please do not grieve
and shed wild tears
and hug your sorrow
to you through the years

Start out bravely
with a gallant smile
and for my sake
and in my name,
live on and do
all things the same

Feed not your loneliness
on empty days,
but fill each waking hour
in useful ways

Reach out your hand
in comfort and cheer,
and I in turn
will comfort you
and hold you near

Never, never
be afraid to die,
For I am waiting
for you in the sky

BY, Helen Steiner Rice

The Beginning:

A Winter Wonderland

A WINTER STORM TRANSFORMED ROCHESTER, New York into a magnificent winter wonderland. Mother Nature flexed her muscles, plummeting a sweet confection of deep, deep snow across the entire area.

While many of her neighbors and friends were lamenting the frightful weather, Jodi Phan was embracing the ethereal beauty before her. She loved the stunning landscape that it created as it covered the bare trees and scenic vistas with a feathery blanket of gleaming whiteness.

Jodi had not seen snow in several years. Her three small children had never seen it. Living in California for the past seven years, Jodi and her husband yearned for the tranquility and enchantment of a New York winter. And this was a true New York winter! Impressive snow drifts rose to meet the tops of front porches and totally enveloped cars with fluffy whitish coverlets. It was a real

New York winter with a chill that made the end of her nose cold to the touch. Jodi wanted to rush outside and feel the snow crunch underneath her feet. She wanted to romp in the snow like she had done as a child, pretending to become frozen in time.

Jodi watched the scenic countryside from her kitchen window. She made herself a steaming mug of hot chocolate, spiking it with tiny multi-colored marshmallows. She took pleasure in the solitude and silence of the serene daybreak. Her only companion was her black Labrador retriever, Mr. Bojangles, who was still resting contentedly on his bed. In the distance, a solitary doe attempted to maneuver about the terrain with great difficulty. Jodi smiled at its efforts to amble through a mass of snow mounds. She had set her alarm clock for six o'clock so that she could enjoy this time alone before her three young children and her husband awakened and interrupted her quiet. It was Sunday and she suspected that church was going to be out of the question. The roads were impassable.

She wouldn't mind if they were all "tucked" in and "hunkered down" for the entire day. But, she was hoping that her children would enjoy the marvel of a frosty winter morning. She would wrap them up warmly in knitted caps, mittens and woolen scarves. She would stuff their tiny feet into hefty boots and immerse them in watertight snowsuits. They would all traipse into the backyard to create snow angels, erect lopsided snowmen and pitch snowballs at bare tree branches and at one another. Hopefully, her little ones would relish the flavor of the season as much as she had when she was their ages. She looked forward to the day ahead.

Perhaps when the roads were cleared, they could venture off to Labrador Mountain, Song Mountain, or the Greek Peak Mountain

Resort for a day of snow tubing. Central New York offered a wealth of opportunities for winter-time excursions. Hibernation was not an option for Jodi. She believed the winter months to be good for the heart and the soul.

She would teach her children how to downhill and cross country ski and to ice skate, snowshoe and fly down the hills on toboggans and sleds. *"What fun!"* she imagined, totally absorbed in the pleasures ahead of them.

She remembered how she learned to ski at Greek Peak, near Cortland, NY over twenty years before. It was so invigorating and exhilarating. Her first time on the slopes, she fell and cried. Her mother came to the rescue with plenty of hugs and lots of advice. *"Why, Jodi," her mother counseled, "you'll soon be soaring down these slopes. If you give up, you will miss so much fun. Don't let life pass you by. Give yourself the chance to try everything physically possible and have fun doing it."* Yes, she had wonderful memories.

It's weird how a song or a scent can trigger a memory.

At that very moment, the smell of the cocoa made her think of her grandmother, her Nonna. Whenever she and her brother and sister spent the night at Nonna's, they were treated to hot cocoa. Instead of the marshmallows, Nonna used to lace their hot chocolate with oyster crackers. The crackers would melt, creating a salty beverage. Then Nonna would draw together her three grandchildren. They would all fit on her lap in a comfortable parlor chair and she would begin telling them stories. Nonna had so many wonderful stories. Jodi remembers all of them. They were all true, not exaggerated. Jodi was proud of her heritage and the

Italian blood that ran through her veins. She was proud of all of the strong women that came before her.

When her cell phone chimed its proverbial ring, she wondered who could possibly be calling her so early in the day. It never occurred to her that the phone call would set in motion a series of unexpected and painful events.

Chapter One:

Tiny Diamonds to Glitter and Dance

MATT HASTINGS LIVED ON A quiet cul-de-sac in a trendy college town neighborhood tucked between the expanse of Cayuga Lake and more than a few picturesque dairy farms. The town's unique makeup came from its location with a breathtaking combination of dramatic hills and lakes. As a doorway to the extensive Finger Lakes Region of New York, the town claimed an endless display of seasonal magnificence. Just minutes from Ithaca and its prestigious Cornell University, there were many historical and cultural activities to keep the residents busy. Its small-town, rural atmosphere, broad, charming tree-lined streets and breathtaking views of hills and valleys made it a warm and inviting place to call "home."

Matt and his wife, Ava owned a lavish two story colonial that was the perfect backdrop for a winter paradise. A February blizzard created a magnificent blanket of glittering whiteness that covered the county. A lush rose and hibiscus garden, currently buried under mounds of snow, separated his home from that of his neighbor Susan Johnson.

On Saturday night after a hearty dinner, Matt and Ava retired early, watching the weather forecast on the television set in their bedroom. They sighed with relief in hearing that the storm that had encompassed the area was losing intensity. Pulling the warmness of the covers over her shoulders, Ava fell asleep first. Turning off the TV, Matt picked up James Patterson's, *Sail* and after several chapters, getting drowsy, he too fell asleep.

Well after midnight, Matt woke up, feeling the urge to go to the bathroom. *"Must have been that last bottle of Heineken I had with dinner,"* he thought as he softly slipped out of bed, hoping not to rouse his wife. Regardless of the furnace kicking on and releasing its warmth throughout the rooms, the night air made the house damp and chilly. Matt pulled a thick, flannel bathrobe from a hook on the bedroom door, he put it on and wrapped it securely around his goose bumped body. *"Ahhhh,"* he smiled, *"That's better."*

As he passed the window looking towards Susan's house, he thought that he saw a silhouette that was impossible to distinguish in front of her garage. It was snowing rather forcefully and he couldn't tell for certain if it was some one or perhaps just a shadow blowing across the back garden. When he finished in the bathroom and passed the window again, he became aware that a light was on in the upper level bedroom. He grinned with embarrassment wondering if Susan had finally found herself a boyfriend. *"Good for her,"* he quipped, slyly.

The next morning the sun peeked its welcoming brilliance out from under the clouds and laid its radiant luster across the white carpet that covered the Earth. Overnight, the skies had cleared, leaving tiny diamonds to glitter and dance across the vastness of white luminosity. The flash of a red cardinal passed before a snow-laden pine tree behind Matt's property. The crystalline glitter of ice sheathed the windowpanes of his home.

In the morning, Ava got up first. She went into the bathroom, brushed her teeth, showered and threw on her well- worn terry cloth bathrobe. Hearing her, Matt woke up and readied himself for the day. Ava began making breakfast. She planned to surprise Matt with a hearty, stick to the ribs morning feast. Matt did not look forward to going outside to face the task of removing the snow piled on top of the ground.

He was ready to relax. He was a college administrator. With the onset of a new semester, it had been a very hectic, demanding week for him. Ava was a critical care nurse at the hospital. This was her first free weekend in the past month. They were looking forward to a carefree, peaceful respite. The snowstorm had put a damper on some of their plans. But, now the couple had a quiet breakfast to look forward to and they both wanted to catch up on their reading and e-mailing. Their four children had fluttered from the nest and were scattered in directions from coast to coast. Their son, Geoff was doing very well as an engineer with a firm in Los Angeles. Recently married, he and his wife had settled in a lovely home in Long Beach. Anna was a teacher in Miami. She and her husband had a three year old son. Matt and Ava's only grandchild was a constant joy. They made frequent trips to Florida to see him. Their son Paul sold real estate in Manhattan. He and his girlfriend lived in a lavish two bedroom condo on

Fifth Avenue and Thirty Second Street. Their youngest daughter, Molly was a law student at Gonzaga University in Spokane. She rented a small efficiency close to the university. They felt very fortunate to have their children in parts of the country that made for exciting vacation destinations. When they retired, they hoped to buy an RV fifth wheel and a diesel truck to hit the road, visiting all of their kids.

After shoveling the remnants of the snowstorm from his driveway, Matt went inside to grab a cup of hot coffee and turn on the radio. His wife was in the kitchen preparing breakfast. The aroma of bacon sizzling in a frying pan made his mouth water. Matt loved to have a breakfast with lots of carbs and sugar on the morning after a big snow. Ava was just breaking eggs into a bowl. Matt noticed a plateful of hash browns next to the stove as he walked into the living room to turn on the radio. Four bagel halves were popping out of the toaster. *"Mmmm,"* he thought, *"A breakfast for a king."*

Adjusting the stations to one that offered the news, he listened. All of a sudden, his heart sank. His confident grin faded into a scowl. *"It can't be,"* he mumbled, lowering the volume. He didn't want Ava to hear the news report. He wanted to tell her face-to-face. Recollections of the evening before burst through his mind. Obviously, he was mistaken about Susan's mysterious caller the night before. Clearly, the light had gone on in Susan's bedroom because she was getting ready to go to Glasswing. Or at least, that is what the radio announcer had said. Matt listened, stunned and saddened to hear that Susan had been in a fatal automobile accident.

"Blizzard like conditions were believed to be the main factor in the death of OCFS teacher, Susan Johnson as her car collided with a pick up truck on highway 15, just outside of Ithaca, two miles from the Glasswing Residential Center in the early hours of Sunday morning."

Ava immediately realized that something was wrong when Matt entered the kitchen. His face was pale and he seemed to be uneasy. He was obviously despairing about something. Walking towards his wife and holding her shoulders firmly, he gave her the painful news. Ava was dazed and overcome with heartache. The fact that Susan had been killed stunned her. Overcome, it was not easy for her to put one foot in front of the other. Not being able to finish making breakfast, she turned off the burner below the bacon. Covering the bowl of beaten eggs and the potato wedges with saran wrap, she set them in the fridge. The bagels stood straight up in the toaster, unattended, waiting for pats of butter and jam.

Matt threw on a Carhart jacket, a pair of work boots, warm gloves and a striped, fleece lined wool cap. Ava ran upstairs and tossed on some jeans and a sweatshirt. Quickly back downstairs, she reached for her Muklucks and also grabbed her long car coat, and mittens and wrapped a tartan flannel scarf about her head. She did not want to be alone in the house. She was too upset. The couple got into their car and drove a few miles to a local convenience store to pick up the Sunday paper, which they trusted would have more thorough information about the accident. As they glimpsed towards Susan's house, nothing looked out of the ordinary. But, a vehicle had left deep tire tracks on the yet unplowed driveway.

Matt took in some air, *"She must have had a real hard time backing out of there with all of the snow on that driveway."*

"Amazing," Ava gasped *"To think, we never heard her leave."* The skid marks from her tires were still on the road in front of the house.

When they arrived at the *Nice and Easy* Store, the cashier, a high school friend of Susan's daughter, acknowledged the Hastings as Susan's neighbors. She broke down.

"I can't believe it," she whimpered, her eyes red and moist with tears. *"Mrs. Johnson was just in here the other day. I remember that she bought cereal and milk. She was all happy and excited about seeing her grandkids and she showed me pictures of them. This is just going to be too much for Jodi with what happened to Amy and all."*

Matt agreed, by shaking his head. He walked around the corner of the counter to steady the young woman, who was obviously shaken. He pulled out a copy of the local *Ithaca Morning Sentinel* from a newspaper holder, put a dollar bill on the cash register and began glancing at the front page.

The newspaper headlines read,

"Winter Storms Socks Area with Snow and Sleet." It went on to state,

"A blustery winter storm dumped over a foot of snow on the area on Saturday and has been blamed for a fatal accident before it blew out of the region early Sunday morning. With gusts up to fifty- five miles an hour, drifted snow on roads created poor visibility for motorists, causing several accidents, including a fatal one. The fierce gusts produced wind chills below zero in most of

the region. Visibility was reduced to a half mile in most areas. New York State trooper Sgt. Jerry Giles reported that slick roads caused the death of Susan Deligrossi Johnson, a local teacher, after she lost control of her 1995 Oldsmobile Cutlass Supreme. Ben Brown the Rehabilitation Director at Glasswing Residential Center recalled Johnson as an outstanding teacher. "On behalf of the entire Glasswing family and the Ithaca community, we lost a great person today and our hearts and prayers go out to Susan and her family," Brown said.

Matt was trembling as he handed over the newspaper to his wife, who was already noticeably upset, sobbing uncontrollably.

"What a tragedy!" Matt exclaimed, giving his wife a tender embrace.

Chapter Two:

Wind, Beneath my Wings!

EARLIER THAT MORNING, CHRISTINA GROVER drove by Susan's house. Christina was a high school teacher in her late forties, pretty and fair- haired with a lightly freckled face. She and Susan had been friends for a long time. They had met at a conference for high school teachers in Albany several years before and found that they had similar interests. They enjoyed camping, canoeing and antiquing together. The two women also treated themselves with a once a year winter spa getaway to the Turningstone Casino in Verona and a summer wine tasting tour of the Finger Lake's Wine trail. Both divorced, they filled their lonely hours with idle chatter, fine dining, glasses of Red Cat, games of BUNKO and church on Sunday mornings. Both of them found it difficult to meet unattached men in Ithaca, so they did not date frequently. Christina had recently convinced Susan to join an on line dating service. Susan was planning to meet one of the men from the service the next week. Christina was amused at how giddy and flighty Susan was about her forthcoming date. Susan and Christina were both keeping their fingers crossed that things would work out on the dating scene for both of them.

The roads had improved some and Christina planned on wrestling the elements to go to church with Susan. She was confident that her Envoy SUV could get them there safely. The good friends usually spent Sunday mornings together. They would attend St. Catherine of Sienna's earliest mass and then pick up a bagel at Collegetown Bagels at the Triphammer Shopping Center. Susan always got decaf and a pumpernickel bagel with vegetable cream cheese. Christina's favorite was high test coffee and a blueberry muffin smothered with creamy butter.

When Christina arrived at Susan's house, she noticed that Susan's car was not parked in the garage. Surprised that her friend did not call her to cancel, she was ready to drive away when she became aware of a note attached to the front door. Luckily, the snow was melted from the sidewalk and she was able to retrieve it easily. The driveway, on the other hand, was still a snow covered mess with huge ruts and cracks all over it. Within a few minutes, Christina's cell phone rang.

Unexpectedly, it was Jodi Phan, Susan's daughter. Amid tears, Jodi told Christina the dreadful news. It was devastating.

"The police called me early this morning," Jodi's voice was barely audible. She was crying uncontrollably. *"Mama's dead! Dead! Oh, God! Help me, Chris! Help me!*

There was a long pause on both ends. Christina could not speak She was petrified, like a statue. So stock-still that she was sure that her heart was not beating.

"You were the first person that I thought to call in Ithaca. We are on our way there. I can't believe this, Chris. I just can't believe it!" The poor girl was sniffling and it was evident that she was holding back her emotions just to get the words out.

Words of anguish and disbelief gushed from Christina's quivering lips. Finally, at last, with some sort of control over herself, she thought to inquire about where Jodi was.

"Are you still in Rochester?" she asked, *"Take your time getting here. The roads are not good. Stay safe and I will see you soon."*

"We are on the thruway. Close to the Weedsport exit" Jodi replied visibly inconsolable. *"Seng and I. The kids are with a neighbor right now. We will be careful. The plows are out. I will see you in about an hour or so. I will need you, Chris."*

"Of course, I'll be here for you. I love you. Bye, hon."

Christina flipped her cell phone closed and threw herself onto the steering wheel. She stayed there, parked in front to Susan's house for what seemed like forever.

Tearfully, Christina read the note that she held in her hand.

Morning Chris,

Too late to call now. May not be back in the morning for church. Off to work to help a kid who needs me. No one else seems to be able to control him. Sorry. See you later. Love, S.

After a few minutes, she gripped the wheel and drove off, crying.

Christina Grover attended the memorial service along with the Hastings and a vast number of other mourners. Jayne Marshall, Susan's very best friend, flew in from the Pacific Northwest.

It was a special woman who could fill a church to overflowing. As the pews of the magnificent Church of the Immaculate Conception were filled to capacity, folding chairs were set up in the vestibules for late arrivals.

Baskets and vases of flowers shrouded the church in arrangements of wreaths, standing sprays, and bouquets of flowers. Redolent, malodorous floral tributes of longiflorum lilies, red, pink and yellow roses, white carnations, and sprays of chrysanthemums and lavender gladiolus bedecked the house of worship. The emotive prayers, poems, and songs in homage of Susan were delivered by inconsolable individuals, who had loved her. Several pictures of her, all showing her cheerful and lighthearted personality, were placed at the altar where the body would normally be. Susan's remains were offered for organ donation. But, her presence was paramount throughout the day. It was a touching service.

When the church's vocalist bellowed out the first few verses of *Wind Beneath My Wings,* Bette Midler's famous song from the movie *Beaches,* everyone understood why the song was chosen for Susan. It encompassed the theme of the movie…enduring friendship, love and support.

'Did you ever know that you're my hero?
You're everything I wish I could be.
I could fly higher than an eagle,
for you are the wind beneath my wings."

Chapter Three:

My Endless Love

BENNY DELIGROSSI SAT IN THE front row of the church, dampened in spirits, empty and brokenhearted. He had a difficult time breathing, trying desperately to hold back his tears. Suddenly, he began to feel the throb of his heart reverberating in his temples. So many memories clouded his mind. Benny, squinting hard to remember, was thinking back to when he and his brother Mikey and sister Susan were just kids. It was over thirty years ago.

He thought it strange that at her funeral, Rob O'Neil suddenly came into his thoughts. Rob was Susan's first love, her forbidden love. Like Romeo and Juliet, the two teenagers were star struck lovers, repeatedly defying their parents by meeting in secret. They were obsessed with each other, desperate to be together and miserable when they were apart. Rob and his wealthy, prominent Irish parents lived on the other side of the tracks from the tightly meshed ethnic Italian neighborhood of the Deligrossi's. Only a few short miles separated them, but they were culturally worlds apart. His father was a banker, hers a barber.

Rob lived on Elm Street, where beautiful, luxurious landscaping highlighted the pristine lawns of large, elegant colonial homes. Rob's neighborhood was serene and peaceful with only the occasional pulsating hum of a solitary lawn mower to carve through the quiet. In contrast, the small, clapboard homes of the Italian neighborhood featured large lawns adorned with religious statues and flamboyant water fountains, surrounded by huge vegetable gardens. Sheets and under garments hung on clothes lines in back yards and the aroma of garlic and onions, fresh baked bread and homemade pasta sauce wafted through the streets. Susan's section of town was flooded with the clamor of women screeching in broken English and high-pitched voices at their children and their boisterous offspring cheerfully squealing back at them. There was the ever constant hubbub of kids gathering on the streets to play stick ball while their fathers came together on bocce ball courts, spluttering cuss words, as they hurled hefty multi colored boccias towards the tiny white pallina.

Susan's family was rough around the edges, rowdy and gaudy. His were refined, controlled and stylish. Rob and Susan were not only separated by the railroad tracks that twisted and turned chaotically across town, but by customs and traditions that created a century long feud.

The Deligossis were hell bent that their only daughter would not date Rob. His parents were equally opposed to Susan.

The Italians and the Irish in their town had quarreled for years. They even worshipped in separate Catholic churches. The one

Catholic cemetery was noticeably divided, alienating them in death, as they had been alienated in life. Their burial grounds became the final reminder of the bad blood between them. The feuds had begun when the two ethnic groups settled as immigrants in Central New York towns working on the Lehigh Valley and Lackawanna Railroad Systems in the late 1800s. The Irishmen were hired to do the most lucrative jobs. They were porters and engineers and ticket masters, wearing starched collars and crisp uniforms. They would gather at their local pubs after work downing glasses of whiskey and frozen tankards of ale. The Italians, however, worked for far less money, laboring at the most unbearable jobs. After working all day, the Italian men flocked to the Sons of Italy Lodge for shots of anisette and bottles of Utica Club.

Susan's own grandfather toiled as a mechanic underneath the big freight cars. Each night, he would walk home from the rail station, his head downcast, his heavy overalls soiled with tar and grease. The crucial difference between the two nationalities, which gave the Irish a tremendous advantage, was their ability to speak the English language. It was also well known throughout the city that when work was sluggish, the Irish were never laid off. The Irish bosses had relatives who owned the Irish pubs, like *The Shamrock* and *O'Toole's* and *O'Malley's*. It would be just plain bad business sense to cut the paychecks of the patrons that spend a lot of money in the pubs.

Susan and Rob's love for one another was doomed to failure. Even though it was all encompassing, beautiful, raw and passionate, it was ill fated. In the end, because of pressure from both families, the two sadly went their separate ways, sooner or later getting married to other people.

Benny knew that Susan had spent many years trying to forget Rob and trying to forgive her father for keeping them apart. She had gone off to college in Pennsylvania. Changed, she some how went off course and detached herself from everyone for a very long time. Benny knew that, even after her marriage to Sean Johnson, she had pined for Rob. Seated there in a church pew at her memorial service, Benny wondered how it might have been if she and Rob had run off together, defying the odds. He, himself, had urged her to end the romance with Rob. Back then, it was all about family and all about respect for their father.

Chapter Four:

In Loving Memory

FOR JODI PHAN, SITTING IN the church, surrounded by her husband and children, her loss was extreme. Trembling, she held on securely to her husband's arm. Unable to accept the reality that her mother was gone to her forever, she was overwhelmed by grief. She and her family had recently moved back to New York from California because Jodi wanted her children to be near their grandmother. Her husband, a doctor, had accepted a position with a local medical practice in Rochester. They were ecstatic to be back relishing in the thought of their first winter in New York. Now, her mother was gone. Fate had certainly thrown them a curve ball.

Leaning forward for a moment to clear her head, she grasped the pew's railing and exhaled noisily, *"Oh, my God!."* She had suddenly remembered something very important! She had remembered that her mother was supposed to meet a man on a blind date.

The arrangements had been made through an on-line dating service. Her mother was so excited about it. After so many years of loneliness, Susan was anticipating a chance to fall in love again. Susan and her mystery man had spoken on the phone several times and she looked forward to their conversations. They seemed to have a lot in common. They were both divorced. They were both Catholic and they seemed to enjoy the same things. Susan's eyes danced when she told Jodi all about the upcoming blind date. Flitting about her bedroom like an elated elf, she breathlessly asked Jodi to help her plan what to wear for her big date. Timidly, she asked her daughter, *"Do you think he will like me?"* Jodi looking closely at her mother, recognized what a very beautiful woman she was. Susan's hair was a bouncy array of brown curls, soft and shiny. Her complexion was flawless with only a few laugh lines around her eyes that scarcely gave away her middle age. Her body was still alluring with firm round breasts that created an ample cleavage that men noticed and loved. She had a full, rounded butt that moved back and forth in a rhythmic motion when she walked. *"He will love you,"* Jodi answered with a smile.

Susan would carry a single red rose so that he would recognize her. *"How romantic,"* Susan blushed. Chatting on and on, she was as fanciful as a teenager, sharing all of the information that she had about him with her daughter.

For the time being, for security reasons, Susan had agreed to only give him her e-mail address. They decided not to exchange names, addresses or any other pertinent information. *"Good."* thought Jodi. She was pleased to see that her mother was being responsible. She smiled to herself, *"It is almost as if our roles have switched.''* She could remember so many times when her mother worried about her dating and staying safe.

Susan's e-mail address was kidsoutwest@yahoo.com, because both of her children lived out west at the time that she picked the address. Michael, Jodi's brother was still in Las Vegas. Her mystery man was RON11047@yahoo.com. Susan began referring to him as RON and he humorously called her KIDS. They made plans to meet at a local Asian restaurant. Susan went on and on.... Ron this and Ron that!

Surfacing back to reality, Jodi shuddered. *"Now what,"* Jodi thought. *"I have to find him and let him know that my mother was not just setting him up to stand him up."* Jodi would go to the restaurant herself to meet RON, explaining why her mother was not there.

Many of Susan's friends and colleagues gave poignant testimonials at her memorial service. Particularly heartrending was an affectionate homage given by one of the inmates from Glasswing.

The youth was tethered in shackles and hand cuffs and guided into the church by two bulky security guards. Wobbling slightly as he stepped up to the pulpit, he cleared his throat several times and then began speaking in broken English, substituting Spanish words here and there. He tenderly offered a thoughtful accolade to Susan. Given special permission to attend the service, the boy spoke in admiration of his former teacher. Every person in the church, frozen to their pew, was sincerely touched as sighs filled the ceremonial chambers of the cathedral. Carlos Montego had given a compelling tribute.

He ended in his native Spanish, *"La Sra. Johnson fue como una madre para mí. Yo la amaba mucho. Descansa en paz, querido maestro. Ahora se siente con Dios."*

Carlos heard that for some reason Miss Johnson was heading to Glasswing for the purpose of helping him. At least, that was the buzz at the facility. He didn't know why she would be doing that. He was doing real well, thanks to her. He had no current problems. Miss Johnson arranged for an anger management program for him and he was putting forth effort to control his temper. For whatever reason, Miss Johnson was not here any more and that broke Carlos's heart.

Chapter Five:

Grown Men Don't Cry

CHICO ALVEREZ PARKED HIMSELF ON the steps of a neglected brownstone at 114th Street and Lexington in Spanish Harlem. He was eating his lunch, chewing the leftovers of a bacalaitos that he picked up at one of the local cuchifrito stands. The popular cod fish fritters were all the rage in his neighborhood. He washed it down with a bottle of Michelob Ultra, wiping remnants of the foam from the beer from his mouth with his hand. Lighting a Marlboro, he took a long deep drag. He had just taken the No. 6 subway train from South Street Seaport back to his apartment in the heart of el barrio, braving the summer subway swelter to make it home in time for a meeting with Jesus Moreno.

A David Henrie look-alike, Chico had a suave and sophisticated demeanor. His jet black hair set the stage for a huge pair of very dark, sexy eyes that lay under thick brows. His lips were plump and his nose was angular. The only facial hair was a small tuft of a mustache. One lonely gold hoop accentuated his right ear lobe.

His jeans were loose fitting, probably a size too large for his long, lean frame. He wore a white t-shirt with an elaborate sketch of a red dragon covering his upper body. He had a small tattoo on his right forearm that almost exactly matched the dragon on his shirt. He wore brown sandals. A blue rope chain encircled his neck. He was good looking and well groomed. The Italian blood flowing through his veins stood out in his chiseled features. But, there was a hint of his Spanish lineage, outlining his mouth and nose.

Oblivious to the massive rumblings of the Metro- North trains and the infectious tempo of the spicy salsa music coming from a store front boom box, Chico tightened his fists, dreading what he was about to do. Flicking the cigarette into the gutter, he took a long deep breath of fresh air.

He waved to several people as they walked past him. He called out, *"Hola. ¡Qué hermoso día de hoy. Ten cuidado."* People respected him. Was it because they liked him or feared him?

He was well- known in el barrio, where he was born twenty years earlier to a Puerto Rican father and a Sicilian mother. Chico's father held two jobs, bartending at *El Cantina Nueva* and playing the guattro in a Puerto Rican trio.

His mother shot up heroin in the back of a pizza parlor just a block and a half from their project. She did every drug she could get her hands on: cocaine, Ecstasy, Oxy Contin and Xanax and she associated with the most horrific street people on the east side of Harlem. She used to be a real beauty, tall and full figured with long, silky brown hair. But, her good looks were stolen from her by the trials and tragedies of her life style. Chico couldn't remember a time when she was there for him. There were no hugs, no nurturing, no tender moments. It was common knowledge that his father had married her because she was pregnant with Chico.

The boy repeatedly suffered from twinges of guilt because he felt to blame for his father's pitiful life with her. He hardly ever thinks about her any more. The last time he saw her, he was six years old and she was being heaved out of the dingy bedroom that she shared with his father by a crusty looking man with a three inch scar running up his left cheek. Chico remembers his father staring off into space, detached and aloof as his wife left them. Chico didn't know where she ended up. He didn't care. But, he did remember her agonizing cries, the repulsive stench of vomit and the way she fleetingly frowned at him with what his father labeled, *"diablo ojos."* She was unfeeling and heartless.

Living with his mother had been intolerable for Chico and his father. His mother's addictions made life a living hell. Things improved when she left, as the root of their pain had been removed. For a short time, he and his father got a long fairly well. His father hauled a lot of junk out of the apartment and took a scrub brush to the walls, floors and bathroom. He scrubbed so hard, it was like he was trying to scrub her out of his mind forever. He fixed the apartment so that it was finally presentable. After cleaning the place up, they took turns doing the housework. Chico's father was an awful cook. Boiling water was a real challenge. The two ate a lot of pizza from a local pizzeria and MacDonald's hamburgers became a staple. Chico became used to preparing frozen dinners in a microwave. He would tell his friends in school, *"We are having a turkey dinner tonight with all of the trimmings."* He neglected to tell them that it came out of a box in a plastic sectioned tray and that it took six minutes in the microwave.

After a year or so, his father married a Puerto Rican woman, named Matilda. She was working at the fish market and when his father started bringing home a bunch of trout and haddock every day, Chico knew something was up. Matilda was years younger than Chico's father. She was petite, curvaceous and attractive. His father lusted after her, like a young Tom Cat in heat. It was Chico's guess that Mattie married the flabby, ornery Mateo Alvarez because she was eager to get her green card and stay in the country. For whatever the reason, Chico was happy that his father was happy. Mattie, as his father called his new wife was an amazing cook and for the first time, the Alvarez men were treated to Bacalodo, a staple of the Puerto Rican diet, which is a flaky, salt-marinated cod fish. They ate it boiled with vegetables and rice or on bread with olive oil for breakfast. They also had plenty of Arroz con pollo, or rice and chicken, served with abichuelas guisada marinated beans, or a native Puerto Rican pea known as gandules. On Sunday afternoons, Mattie served up bowls of asopao, a rice and chicken stew. Her specialties also included lechón asado, slow-roasted pig; pasteles, meat and vegetable patties rolled in dough made from crushed plantains; empanadas dejueyes, Puerto Rican crab cakes; rellenos, meat and potato fritters; griffo, chicken and potato stew; and tostones, battered and deep fried plantains, served with salt and lemon juice. Chico and his father often washed down with cerveza rúbia, "blond" or light-colored American lager beer, or ron the world-famous, dark-colored Puerto Rican rum. Mattie provided mouth-watering meals for them. Chico knew that Mattie was good for his father and his father's life was much more comfortable with his new wife by his side.

But, there was little harmony or cordiality between Chico and his step-mother. She judged him as second-rate because of his Sicilian heritage. To her all Sicilians were junkies or drunks, stupid and lazy- mafioso. His mother certainly filled the bill. Chico became ashamed of his heredity and as a result, he was at odds with Mattie all of the time. They argued relentlessly and she continually badgered and humiliated him. When he was fifteen and he couldn't take the condemnation and criticism any longer, he busted out of there. Mattie's words to him as he slammed the door behind him ripped at his heart, *"Riddens buena para usted. Vaya, es un inútil hijo de puta Ir!"* The fact that his father let him walk out, wounded him.

Initially, he was without a roof over his head, living off the charity of others, begging and hustling for every morsel of food and every bit of loose change. Chico became a "kid living on the edge." In due course, he did whatever he had to do to stay alive on the streets. He would lift food from the local bodega and cigarettes from gas stations. When that became effortless for him, he began to pocket money from unsuspecting women, assaulting them for whatever cash they had in their purses. Finally, he graduated to armed robbery, stealing larger sums of money from local merchants and even a bank or two.

Consequently, he fell into the gang network, joining the Netas, a Puerto Rican street gang, which had connections to inmates in the prisons and detention centers in New York State. He was on the fast track and because he was smart and feisty, he became more and more prominent with the gangs. Chico spent a few months in one of the Youth Residential Centers in Upstate New York and while incarcerated, he became more caught up with hard core criminals.

This led to his dealing drugs and pimping street- based prostitutes. Carlos had numbed his emotions beyond human touch and because everything he loved was taken from him, he erected a wall to separate himself from his pain and turned himself into a man with no human emotion, pity or compassion for the human race. He no longer had the ability to love, hate, desire or despair. Before his nineteenth birthday, Chico Alvarez was killing people for money. He was the Netas" number one hired gun and he was damn good at what he did.

That is precisely why Jesus Moreno called on him. Chico knew that no one ever said, *"No"* to Jesus Moreno and in essence, whatever Jesus wanted Jesus got on a silver platter. This job was going to be very different and he regretted it before it even happened. Several years before, Jesus had asked Chico to do a job for him. That one hit home. As he dumped the beaten, bloody carcass into the Hudson, he thought about his own tormenting demons. He had a monster for a parent, too.

Chapter Six:

The Sins of the Father

EXCEPT FOR A FEW TRIPS to Miami, Puerto Rico and Vegas, Jesus Moreno had spent every single day of his twenty - five years huddled up in the northeast corner of Manhattan, adjacent to the Harlem River and en route to the legendary Bronx. Jesus got his mother out of el barrio, but he did not intend to leave there himself. To him, it was his home and his life line. He never received a complimentary round trip to Glasswing or Underwood or Clearview or one of the other Upstate Juvie Centers. Just about everyone he knew had been "locked" up somewhere in the Finger Lake's Region. But, Jesus was too clever to get caught and it helped that he had a few crooked cops in his corner.

Jesus was short, only 5'6" with a broad, hefty frame. He looked much heavier than his 176 pounds. He was dark skinned with pleasant, undefined features. His hair was cut close to his scalp and a dark five o'clock shadow damned his oval shaped face. He wore no jewelry at all. His left arm and back were adorned with colorful tattoos, mostly Asian in origin.

He always dressed well with Prada dress shirts, Armani sweaters, Dolce and Gabbana jeans, Gucci Tees and he would never leave his house without his Rolex Air King fluted bezel time piece. Jesus was chic and classy. He dressed to impress. He did everything with style, including driving his black Benz all over the hood.

Even his girl friend was flashy and flamboyant. Angelina was a topless hostess in a strip bar before Jesus took her away from that sordid lifestyle and set her up in a condo to be his very own "juguete amor," or love toy. She was hot and sexy and she didn't mind showing it. She had the best of everything; the finest clothing and footwear, the most discriminating foods and wines, lavish jewelry, pricey hair styles and manicures, and luxury vacations. In return, she was available for Jesus whenever he saw fit. There were times when he wanted her all to himself and times when he would take her out on the town, showing her off as his "trophy woman." She never met his mother. She never would. Women like Angelina were not proper enough to meet this mother.

But all of the material possessions in the world could not disguise his sadness. He was sad from his earliest memories. In fact, he had very few memories of his childhood. All those memories that most people cherish and look back on were the ones that Jesus had suppressed, hiding them some place far away.

What he did remember, however, were his father's visits. They were very infrequent, once every two or three months. His father was gone on business trips for several weeks at a time. As soon as the man encroached on them, he would take over the couch, bark out commands to Jesus's mother, raid the fridge and begin snapping the taps off beer cans, one after the other, until the trash was filled with the stale smelling leftovers. The man would also chain smoke, leaving a trail of nasty cigarette butts in every ashtray in the Moreno home. It got to a place that whenever Jesus heard that snapping sound of beer cans, he would shy away, hiding in his bed, covering his face with a thick quilt. As soon as the beer was gone, his father would start gnashing and sucking his discolored teeth.

Soon after that, his mother would be shrieking in pain. His father would pull her hair, kick her, slap her and force himself on her. The violent behavior would continue all through the night. When little Manuela began to shed tears, Jesus would soothingly remove his baby sister from her crib and place her into his bed, holding her securely until morning. He would watch over her as her huge coffee colored eyes began to get heavy and she fell sound asleep. He was determined to shield her from the brutality of their cruel father and from any one else who would ever try to harm her. He hated those visits. He hated his father.

There was something that Jesus just could not figure out. When his father got tired of them and went on his way, his mother gathered her children about the big oak table in the dining room. She would look at them with her puffed-up eyes and in a quaking voice she would caution them,

"Your papa is a good man. He doesn't mean what he does to me. Sometimes, it is my fault. I do things that make him wild."

"No way" Jesus cried. *"No way. De ninguna manera. Él es un borracho cobarde y voy a matarlo."* Running from the table, he left his mother and sister sitting there, both troubled by his response.

It wasn't until years later, when Jesus was grown, that the roles reversed. There came a time when the elder Moreno was terrified of his son. There came a time when he didn't bother them any more.

When the county sent Manuela to Brentwood, Jesus tried pulling rank. The judge was a real hard nose. He wouldn't set bail and she got a year for soliciting Johns on the Boulevard. Jesus didn't know that she was turning tricks. She was just a kid. She was thirteen years old when they rolled her off. She was fourteen when he identified her stone- cold body in the morgue on 118th Street. She was only home from Brentwood for three days when her pimp had her wasted for talking to the jakes. It broke his mother's heart. Jesus was determined to get retribution and settle the score with every one responsible for hurting his sister.

At her funeral, there was a chill in the air, a gentle rain and a solemn silence, which created a somber stage for the mourners, who were sheltered beneath a procession of black umbrellas. Jesus balanced his wavering, unsteady body by holding on tightly to the foundation of an old elm tree, sobbing hysterically.

"They will pay for this," Jesus promised her. *" No te preocupes, hermanita. Los haré pagar por lo que han hecho a usted."*

That was a year ago. He was waiting, biding his time, refining his options, getting all of his ducks in order. He was patient. He was powerful. He was the one holding the stacked deck. He had a list of people to hold responsible and the list was getting longer.

Chico was meeting him at the pawn shop. It was safe there. They could make their plans without being bothered.

Chapter Seven:

If I Only Had A Heart

MANUELA MORENO AND JULIA VALDEZ knew each other forever. They were best friends and so were their mothers before them. Both Juanita Moreno and Consuela Valdez were pregnant at the same time, both hoping for little girls. Juanita had a five year old son, Jesus and Consuela, a three year old, Victor. The women delivered their daughters three days apart and the little girls were the best of playmates. In spite of the fact that both girls had deadbeat, losers for fathers, they had grown into happy, well adjusted children.

Both girls were the shining stars in their families. Their older brothers adored their little sisters and were their steadfast protectors. Both, Manuela and Julia were cheerful, intelligent, compassionate and gentle adolescents. But, most of all, they were innocent children. Unlike many of the other girls in their neighborhood, Manuela and Julia did not get into any trouble. They were not, yet, interested in boys and they both had plans to go to college and follow their dreams. They both wanted to pursue careers in fields that would benefit others. Manuela was planning on becoming a social worker and Julia had wanted to go to nursing school.

It was a day like every other day in el barrio. The cool, crisp September air of New York City gently hit them by surprise as they drew their sweaters firmly around their shoulders. Manuela and Julia were walking home from Saint Anne's Parochial School, where they had both been honored with full scholarships. The girls, clad in traditional catholic school uniforms of navy blue and white plaid jumpers, brown saddle shoes, crisp white button down collared blouses and navy blue cardigans were chatting with gleeful amusement, not paying much interest to anything going on around them.

Manuela was the gregarious, vivacious one. She was tall and long legged, at least two inches taller than her older brother. She had a pretty face with large dimples that stayed put even when she wasn't laughing. Her hair, which was secured neatly at the back of her neck with a navy scrunchy was a chestnut color, long and lush and her eyes were light brown with speckles of gold floating and glistening amid the pupils. Her childhood body had formed into a curvy, shapely one. Her uniform fit snuggly about her enlarging breasts. She was a beauty, a rare treasure. Manuela's idol was Jennifer Lopez, a famous Latina actress and it was uncanny how much Manuela looked like the famous star.

Julia, on the other hand, was bashful and reserved. She was adorable with short, cropped black hair, parted in the center and adorned with two white hair clips. Her large emerald green eyes dazzled when she smiled. She was tinier than Manuela, slender and lanky. Her uniform fit loosely about her gangling frame. She had not begun to develop a womanly shape. She looked and acted younger than her thirteen years, caught somewhere between being a child and a woman. She was an angelic little wisp of a child, fairylike. As they drew near the traffic circle, Julia glided her arm tenderly under Manuela's and they strolled arm and arm, laughing nervously, drifting from side to side, harmoniously.

It had been such a good day at school. The friends had both received excellent report cards. They were also chosen to have key roles in the school play, *Wizard of Oz*. Manuela had landed the role of Dorothy and Julia was going to have the part of the Tin Man. As they walked gingerly through the streets, they began singing, "*Somewhere Over the Rainbow.*" Then Julia, who had practiced her solo, chimed in with the famous song from *Wizard of Oz*,

"When a man's an empty kettle he should be on his mettle, And yet I'm torn apart.
Just because I'm presumin' that I could be kind-a-human,
If I only had heart.
I'd be tender - I'd be gentle and awful sentimental
Regarding Love and Art.
I'd be friends with the sparrows ...
and the boys who shoots the arrows
If I only had a heart.
Picture me - a balcony. Above a voice sings low.
Wherefore art thou, Romeo? I hear a beat....
How sweet.

Just to register emotion, jealousy - devotion,
And really feel the part.
I could stay young and chipper '
and I'd lock it with a zipper,
If I only had a heart."

The girls both laughed hysterically when Julia finished her song. *"Great job! Great job! Tin man!"* Manuela praised her friend excitedly. Julia merrily hopped up and down, smiling from ear to ear.

They were both delighted with the opportunity to be in the play. Anxious to tell their mothers the great news, they began to walk more quickly. But, the good day they were having soon turned into a nightmare.

It turned out to be a triple tragedy. Jimmy Dentes was driving his red Chevy S10 pickup truck from the high school. He was on his way to his after school job at the pharmacy on 117th Street. He was another barrio success story. Jimmy was an honor student, an athlete and overwhelmingly popular with the girls. Handsome, the girls in his high school affectionately compared him to the actor, Matt Damon. He enjoyed playing baseball. He characterized himself as a good ballplayer who excelled around the diamond. He pitched and also played catcher and third base — a jack of all trades, if you will. He was a strong-minded young man, who had an opportunity for an academic scholarship to Cornell University in their Vet School. He loved animals and every stray cat that he could find, he sheltered, pampered and nurtured. Things were going well for him. He and his girlfriend, Anita were happy together and she had her own ambitions that paralleled his. She planned on four years at Buffalo University and then law school, if all went well. But as fate would have it, in a matter of seconds, Manuela and Jimmy's lives would be torn apart, their dreams shattered and Julia would lay dead, face down on a cold cement sidewalk.

Jimmy had no idea that when he answered his mobile phone and attempted to respond to a text message from his girlfriend, that his truck would veer right into the two girls. It seemed that he took his eyes off the road for only a few seconds. Manuela sustained minor injuries. She had some scratches and bruises and a sprained wrist. But, her screams were deafening. The brunt of the impact fell on Julia. She was gone, killed instantaneously. The picture of her young, motionless body lying there would haunt both Manuela and Jimmy for the rest of their lives.

Jimmy would not be going to Cornell. He would be trading an Ivy League education for four years at Walton Correctional Prison, sixty miles from home. He was eighteen years old, adjudicated as an adult, convicted of vehicular manslaughter.

Manuela was beaten to the bone by what took place that day. At the funeral, which was held in the Church of the Holy Rosary at 444 East 119th St. in New York City's East Harlem, Manuela was numb, except for a steady dull pain in her chest and the cadenced throbbing of her wounded heart. She didn't want to feel. She wanted to escape. She wanted to join Julia. She found it difficult to breathe and she held on firmly to her brother's hand all through the service. *"If I only had a heart,"* she whimpered, exhaling loudly.

Chapter Eight:

Torn to Shreds

MANUELA WAS EVAPORATING, ONE DAY at a time. She was escaping into a world which was hopeless and desperate.

Her profound melancholy intensified as the weeks passed. She felt that school, friendships, and other parts of her life were put on hold for the foreseeable future. She felt miserable all of the time and laden with heartache. She lost interest in all the activities that up to that time she had enjoyed. Her grades plummeted. She never showed up for play rehearsals, relinquishing the part of Dorothy. Her loss of appetite, her insomnia, and her feelings of worthlessness and excessive guilt disturbed her family intensely. Manuela's destructive behavior was devastating, not only to herself, but to every one around her. They watched over her closely for signs of suicide. Manuela wanted the world to go away. She wanted to hide from reality. And for her, reality did fade away one day at a time.

Six months after Julia's death, Manuela met Darren Reed, a twenty- five year old street hustler. He was devious and crafty, street wise and ruthless. Known as "the King" in the hood, Darren plucked young girls off the streets, enticing them into prostitution by promises of nice clothes, money and shelter. Reed was a snake who stalked the streets for his prey, hunted them down and ate them alive. Manuela's state of vulnerability put her right in the palm of his leachy paws. She began spending more and more time with Reed and his crew of hoodrats, avoiding school and family. Reed was persuasive when he told her how much he wanted to protect her. Her state of confusion and mental turmoil, overshadowed any sense of right and wrong. And through that association, Manuela Moreno started turning tricks on New York City's East Side. It was a grim, sordid and unsafe existence. She knew that. However, for some reason even as loathsome as he was, she held on tightly to Darren Reed.

Even though her family was frightened for her, they had no idea that she had taken up with such revolting and repulsive people. They surely had no idea that she was a street walker. They finally found out when she was busted by an undercover cop who spotted her on a corner. The cop was sure that the trashy, shoddy clad kid was a hooker. After soliciting her, the cop cuffed her, the judge sentenced her and she was sent to Brentwood Residential Center in Upstate NY.

At her court hearing, she was torn apart knowing that she had wounded her mother. Her heart wrenched when her mother entered the courtroom. The look that passed between them was one of hopelessness. Manuela could tell that her mother was still in denial over what had happened to her daughter. The judge showed no mercy. Manuela believed that he treated her like the dirt bag that she had turned into. She took a deep breath as she saw her mother fishing in her purse for a hankie to wipe her tears. Jesus was there, gaping off into the distance. He was helpless when the judge turned down his proposals. There was nothing he could do.

"No bail. It is in her best interest," the judge, raising one eyebrow, told Jesus in a harsh, uncompromising manner.

After Manuela was arrested, she was quickly buzzed into a holding station for three days. The place reeked of disinfectant. While there, she had her picture taken from every angle. Those mug shots revealed unhappiness, anguish and pain. She was forced to put nasty green stuff in her hair to kill lice, which she didn't have and she was ordered to take a quick shower in front of female correctional officers. Their improper stares enraged her. She cried when they strip searched her, wondering how in the hell she could ever put anything in the places that they looked. It was humiliating, even for a girl who had been a prostitute. She met with a stern, stiff faced medical nurse who took her blood, jabbing her hard in the arm and gave her a half ass physical exam. The nurse asked her if she had any STD's, AIDS, or Hepatitis-C. Then she tested her for tuberculosis, jabbing her hard, again.

Under the harsh glare of overhead fluorescence, a bald headed intake case manager with a military demeanor asked her a horde of questions.

"Did she have any gang affiliations?"

She said that she did not. She wondered if she should have mentioned that Jesus was a Neta.

"Was she a homosexual?"

She swallowed hard. These questions were so embarrassing.

"Who would be visiting her first?"

She didn't know. It would most likely be her mother.

Groggy and disoriented from all of the questioning, Manuela shook her head from time to time to clear her thoughts. Because of the nature of her crime, the judge had required intense psychological screening, which would begin when she got to Brentwood. They wanted to start immediate treatment for depression, stress and anxiety.

A few weeks later on a raw October morning, Manuela found herself on a bus, the only passenger being transferred to Brentwood in Central New York. She had never been away from the ghetto before. She braced herself as the bus hit some bumpy rural roads. For a while, rain hammered against the windows, causing the wipers to flare into a steady, rhythmic beat. Swish! Swish! Her mind was speeding to another place, another time.

The metrical rhythms of the wipers eased her racing mind. When the rain stopped, she began to enjoy the trip through beautiful farm country. She was in awe of the beautiful scenery that they passed. Manuela was amazed at the marvelous rolling hills and the colors of the exploding fall foliage, a kaleidoscope of brilliance. As they drove down quiet country roads, she was drawn to the lovely farms framed with large pastures and fruit orchards. She savored the majestic views and momentarily escaped into an imaginary world. She saw herself, splashing in the crystal clear ponds, running through the vast countryside, and skipping up the gravel roads towards velvet meadows and blueberry bushes, highlighted with dazzling panoramic views surrounded by vibrant landscapes of historic farmsteads and open fields. She marveled at the beautiful farm houses with their large, wrap around country porches, quaint red barns and the gorgeous appeal of manicured grounds. She felt as if she was immersed in a storybook.

She had never seen a real cow before. And now she saw cows, lots of cows. She never realized that they came in so many color combinations and patterns. Finally arriving at her destination. she was sorry that the trip was over. With her imaginary trek through the countryside interrupted by the sharp contrast of the austere prison in front of her, Manuela was wrenched back into the real world. She dreaded what was ahead of her.

Brentwood was depressing, dark and gloomy. Exiting the bus with some assistance from the driver. She was waist shackled and struggled to get her balance. She walked with difficulty. Once in the building, she was greeted by some abrasive and harsh individuals. They began shouting instructions and regulations at her. Her head was spinning.

The corrections officers tossed dungeon clothes at her. A red and yellow jumpsuit, seven pair of white underpants, four white bras, seven pair of white socks and a pair of white kicks made up her new wardrobe. She was also given a musty smelling bed roll, a tube of toothpaste, a toothbrush, deodorant, a comb, a hair brush and bath and hand soap, three towels and three wash cloths. After being fingerprinted, she was thrown into a holding cell with a bunch of smelly crack heads, who shot her hard, vile looks. It terrified her. Finally, after a few days, she was assigned to a room with another resident in one of the thirty or forty cottages that were scattered about the grounds.

Her room was sparsely furnished. Two plastic covered mattresses that smelled like disinfectant sat on top of two wooden platforms. There was one desk, a toilet, a wash basin and some plastic crates for her clothes. Her roommate was gone. She was in a therapy session. Manuela was glad that she didn't have to deal with any one. She was tired and confused. A few moments of peace and quiet was what she yearned for. She basked in the silence for several moments before beginning to settle into what would be her new home for quite some time. She took a pillow, an army blanket and some sheets out of her bedroll and began to make her bed. Then she sat on the bed, wondering how she got to this place. That night, she prayed to Julia. *"Please, help me survive this horrible place."* She didn't pray to God any more. He had abandoned her.

Bad memories of Julia's death came back at to her unexpectedly. She felt the same fear and horror that she did when the event took place. She felt like she was going through the event over and over again. This, she learned, was called a flashback. Sometimes there was a trigger, a sound or sight that caused her to relive the event. She had lived through a dreadful experience which resulted in other dreadful experiences. She was a chaotic mess. They needed to help her and do it swiftly to circumvent an attempted suicide. Her therapists worked with her methodically day after day. What helped her the most was writing and rewriting her experiences into a memoir. It helped to move nightmares and intrusive thoughts into her past. It didn't cure the PTSD, but it made life more endurable.

The medical staff at Brentwood had no choice but to prescribe Zoloft, which helped with her depression. It was a long, long lonely and friendless road to recovery.

She soon came to realize that Brentwood was not such an awful place. It was staffed with very caring and dedicated people. At Brentwood, she wasn't alone. Many people were there for her. They truly cared about her. Manuela's teachers and counselors saw potential. With counseling and one-on-one tutoring, Manuela inch by inch came out of the shell that encapsulated her bruised and tarnished soul. Symptoms of post traumatic disorder had disrupted her life, making it hard to continue with her daily activities. But, she was getting better. She began to believe again....in herself and in God. Watching her metamorphosis was a wonderful thing.

She began to heal. Opening up, she talked and talked and talked. Everything that she knew about the despicable Darren Reed was put out there. That, however, was a calamitous mistake!

Chapter Nine:

A Teacher Affects Eternity

SUSAN DELIGROSSI JOHNSON WAS GETTING her life back together. The attractive, slender, brunette had suffered some major, horrifying set backs in the recent years. It took every bit of self control and fortitude for her to withstand the pain of losing her daughter, Amy, to a devastating heart condition. She was still having tremors from the quakes of a nasty divorce. Her elderly mother was suffering from dementia and her life was hitting rock bottom. But, willfully, she took the bull by the horns and started to take her life back. She had grit and courage. She focused on the blessings in her life. She still had a beautiful daughter, Jodi, a wonderful son, Mike and some amazing treasures in her grandchildren. She was devoted to her brother Benny and she leaned on him for support. She lived in a lovely home in a pleasant neighborhood in the beautiful Finger Lakes Region of New York. Susan had many good, genuine friends and she was even beginning to date again. Trusting men was an issue. But, she would take baby steps and hopefully, they would turn into giant strides.

Susan's personal accomplishments came from her job as a teacher at a residential facility for young men, ages thirteen to eighteen. The boys were there for a lot of different reasons. Many of them were drug offenders with a penchant for using and abusing any drug they could get. Others were in detention for burglary, DUIs, sexual offenses and other felony charges.

In spite of what her students did in the past, she loved her job and she loved teaching them. Susan had the philosophy that *"no kid was born bad."* She believed that with attention and love, nine times out of ten the kids in her classes wanted to do the right thing. She offered a classroom, where they could relax, feel comfortable and be respected. She expected a lot from her students and they more often than not delivered.

Susan taught them more than academics, she taught them good manners, grooming, parenting skills, financial planning and independent living skills, including cooking and sewing lessons. *"Miss Johnson was like a mom to me,"* one of her students informed the school's principal. *"Kids show her love because she loves them back. They don't get no better than her."*

Susan worked long hours every day just to guarantee that her "boys" had all that they needed to achieve well on tests and to do their homework successfully. *"Very few people are given the opportunity to watch these kinds of children grow and develop and know that they have played an important part in that process,"* she used to tell others. Her students came to her cloaked in years of failure, downtrodden by overwhelming, bigger-than-life problems.

Susan loved her rewarding life, for her belief was that the greatest use of life is to spend it on something that outlasts it…her students, her boys.

Susan promised herself that she would work to make a difference. She implored God to show her the way. She needed a sign to confirm that the path that she had taken at Glasswing was the right one. That sign did not come in a bolt of lightening or a stream of shooting stars or a blare of rockets. It came in one boy and the fact that he shared a birthday with Amy. Carlos Montego was born on August 15, 1981, the same day and year that her little girl was born. It was a holy day in the Catholic Church, the "Feast of the Assumption of the Blessed Virgin Mary." The church believed that those born on a holy day were special, somehow blessed. Susan saw it as a sign. Amy and Carlos, both special, both hers to help.

She worked hard at helping all of the boys and she especially worked hard at helping Carlos. He was struggling. His behavior was unpredictable. His grades were inconsistent. His mood swings were up-and-down. He was fragile. Susan was determined to help him become all that he was capable of becoming. She knew that Carlos could not go back to his old neighborhood. He was in trouble with the gang network and they were going to kill him if he went back. Susan was working very hard at trying to give him another option. She and the placement counselors were hopeful that they would be able help him find a foster home some place downstate, where he could have a fresh start. Some place where no one knew him. Some place where his potential would be discovered. Some place where he could stand out and excel.

It was a personal badge of achievement for her every time one of her kids did well on a test, passed a GED, found a decent job out in the world, or left the center with the option to go to college. She was their mentor, their supporter, their biggest advocate and their friend. Susan was also very much valued by the other teachers and the administration. She had received a number of recognitions and awards from the State of New York and the people in Albany highly praised her hard work. The horrendous accident that took her life on an abandoned stretch of highway that was prone to heavy drifting snow, fog and freezing rain, shocked the entire OCFS community.

Chapter Ten:

When Tigers Eat their Young

DARREN REED KNEW EXACTLY WHEN Manuela Moreno was getting out of lock up. He knew everything that went on in all of the detention centers. He had his contacts. He had some paid acquaintances and then he had the snitches who just wanted to get on his good side. Usually, they were former street walkers who wanted to be part of his crew in East Harlem. He also knew that Manuela had betrayed him. She had given the authorities a lot of names, numbers and other information and he was not going to let her get away with that. Her days were numbered. No one screws around with the King.

He didn't even want it to look like an accident. He wasn't worried about going under the radar with this one. He wanted everyone in the hood to know exactly who was responsible. This was going to be a lesson for everyone on the streets. He wanted all his girls to get the message that if you mess with the King, pay back will be painful.

What Darren didn't bargain for was that Jesus, Manuela's older brother was moving up in the world of the Netas, one of the fiercest, most corrupt and powerful street gangs in the hood. As shady, sly and devious as he was, himself, Darren Reed was about to meet his match and make a colossal error in judgment.

Manuela was ready to go home after a year and three months at Brentwood. She was anxious to see her mother and to go back to school. On the day that she was to leave, all of the teachers, psychologists, nurses, corrections officers and social workers were their to say their, *"goodbyes"* and to give her their best wishes. She was beaming. Her self confidence was back and she felt wonderful; happy and fortunate to be given a second chance. Her return bus trip to the Bronx was exhilarating. This time, she was free of the weight of chains. Manuela was able to exhale for the first time in a very long time. Remembering the beauty of the area, she pleadingly asked the bus driver several times to stop along the way.

"Please, we are really in no rush," she begged. *"I just want to enjoy the rural areas for awhile."*

"Well, actually we do have to get back. I am on a pretty rigid schedule." the driver informed her. *"But, I think we can stop for a little while. It is beautiful here."*

Even though it was against the rules, he agreed because she was so excited to experience everything. Getting off the Interstate as cars and eighteen wheelers swished by them, the driver treated her to a back road panoramic adventure. He guided her through rolling mountain terrain, breathtakingly beautiful waterfalls, thriving woodlands and miles of winding rivers. She even got out of the bus to get nose to nose with a lone dairy cow. Giggling and dancing about like a leprechaun, Manuela treasured every incidence as if she would never live it again. The driver, himself, normally a cantankerous workaholic, became cheerful and lighthearted. They were both enjoying their romp through the meadows and valleys, villages and townships.

Chapter Eleven:

A Single Rose

MANUELA PLANNED ON IGNORING DARREN Reed when she got home. She was going to go back to school and make things better for every one that loved her. She was going to use all of the coping skills and counsel and guidance that she received at Brentwood to her benefit and she was going to honor Julia's memory by moving forward in a path that would lend a hand to others in need.

She realized how sick she had been and now that she was better, nothing was going to stop her from making up for her losses.

As soon as she got back to the Bronx, she registered at her old school, a bit embarrassed to see her teachers again. Miss Johnson wrote copious letters of recommendation for her so that she could continue there on scholarship. She was sure that her criminal records were expunged because of her juvenile status. But, when a kid in Spanish Harlem is gone from school as long is she was, it usually means a detention center. Besides, not much stays a secret in her neighborhood. Most of the kids that come out of lock up are proud that they did time. It is some kind of power trip for them. But, not Manuela. To her, it was exactly as it was, a disgrace.

She missed Julia a lot. But, she was coping with that loss. She realized that Julia's death was not her fault. It was something that she had no control over. She could mourn Julia, but not blame herself. In the past, she had faulted herself for not stepping in front of Julia, pushing her aside and taking that crushing blow.

As much as she tried, she couldn't hide from Darren Reed. He calculated her very move. He knew where she was every minute. Soon after she got home, she lost her life the same way that Julia did. But, this time it was no accident. Within five minutes after she died, the word on the streets was that Darren Reed had a local junkie in a red Toyota Tundra plow into her right in front of her own house.

When the word got back to Susan that Manuela had been killed, it broke her heart. She loved that girl as if she were her own daughter. She wanted to attend Manuela's funeral in the Bronx. But, it was an OCFS regulation that state employees not have any contact with former students or their families. As an alternative, she had a tree planted on the grounds at Brentwood in Manuela's memory. It was a lovely Rose of Sharon tree or *Althea Hibiscus*, which created loads of double blossoms. Susan placed a modest plate below the tree, which was inscribed with:

> *A single rose can be my garden... a single friend,*
> *my world. ~Leo Buscaglia*
> *Two friends. One life, lost too soon.*
> *In loving memory of Manuela*

In the late summer, Manuela's tree was covered with bubble-gum pink flowers that were so "double" they looked like carnations. Susan loved to watch the hummingbirds and butterflies swarm around the tree. What a beautiful tribute to a beautiful young lady!

Jesus Moreno was waiting. Unlike, Darren Reed, he was not going to be impatient. Things would happen on his turf in his time. And, no one would ever link him to it. No, Jesus was going to play it safe. He didn't want any free trips to prison. He was not about to hurt his mother. Jesus Moreno was smart.

Chapter Twelve:

Hit With a One- Two Punch

JODI PHAN WAS RESTLESS EVER since her mother's funeral. She was plagued with fitful nightmares and she felt convinced that her mother was trying to reach her. Her husband prescribed some medication for her to help her sleep and to calm her anxiety. Unfortunately, nothing seemed to reduce the onset of bizarre and prevailing feelings of her mother's presence in her home. It did not frighten her. But, it was uneasy in the sense that she felt more and more every day that something was disturbing about the way her mother died. She was also plagued with the thought that she had an unfinished matter to attend to. She had to get together with the mysterious stranger that her mother had intended to meet at the Asian restaurant.

But, before she met with her mother's mystery man, she had to go through the gloomy, unpleasant task of going through her mother's possessions. She was adamant on doing it alone. While unpacking a few boxes that were thronged together on the top shelf of Susan's closet, she came across an ornately festooned hat box. Susan was soon to realize that the box held the memories that were the caretakers of her mother's heart.

In the box, were several snapshots of her and of Michael and Amy. There was one of Michael grinning excitedly as he was building sand castles on the white, talcum powdered beaches of Destin, Florida. There was one of a toothless Amy proudly donning a pink, ruffled Easter dress, displaying a large brightly bejeweled stuffed bunny. Looking at that picture closely, Jodi had almost forgotten how Amy's magnificent blue eyes were almost iridescent.

There was one of herself, wearing a dazzling lapis blue cocktail dress, holding on to the arm of a gawky, acne faced prom date. She remembered that day so vividly. Her mother was all a flutter over the prom dress and the hairdo and the jewelry. Jodi, herself, was not quite as excited about it all. The picture revealed her lack of enthusiasm.

There was one of her and Michael cheerfully tearing into gaily wrapped Christmas packages. There was one of all three of the Johnson children, wearing Mickey Mouse ears in front of Cinderella's Castle at Disney World. There was Amy blowing out twelve candles on a sumptuously adorned birthday cake. *"That was her last birthday,"* Jodi reminisced, thoughtfully.

As Jodi dug deeper, she came across several letters written in the shaky, undeveloped script of children with misspelled promises of love. One from Michael was adorned with pieces of elbow macaroni.

There was one from Jodi which featured a white lace heart-shaped paper napkin attached to red construction paper. Amy's was a drawing of a huge, yellow sun with a smiley face. There were also quite a lot of frilly, lacey, poetic anniversary cards from her father. They all professed eternal devotion. Jodi found it strange that her mother would keep them.

She also discovered wedding pictures, tucked in beneath the anniversary cards. Yellowing with age, the photos were of a happy time. They showed a radiant bride dressed in an elegant white satin wedding gown and a long floor length veil attached to a gladiola swathed Juliet cap. Her generous spray of gladiolas was held with both hands.

Her handsome new husband, who wore a fashionable tuxedo stood beside her, holding her arm affectionately. Another photo revealed the whole wedding party. Everyone was smiling broadly. The maid of honor was wearing a light pink gown with a crimson colored bolero jacket and she clutched a luscious bouquet smothered with pink and powder blue carnations.

Her mother's attendants were dressed in light powder blue gowns with navy blue bolero jackets. They carried powder blue and pink carnations. The groomsmen wore navy blue tuxedos and pink, ruffled dress shirts with crimson colored bow ties. In another, the young couple was flanked on both sides by their proud parents.

The fathers were beaming and the mothers were smiling freely. Jodi sucked in a large amount of air as she imagined how exultant her mother was that day, anticipating a joyful future.

Subsequently, way at the bottom of the heap, buried somehow amid the good stuff was a small brown, paper bag, held firmly together with a frayed red string. Jodi very carefully untied the string, thinking that whoever had put it into the bag was making it very difficult for her to open it. Inside she came across an envelope, which had been folded neatly in half. Her mother's name and address pranced across it in a wavering handwriting that she instantly recognized as her father's. She closed her eyes, feeling a large lump form in the back of her throat. She felt as if she was about to listen in on a very private tête-à-tête. Jodi carried the letter carefully between two fingers as if it were a bomb ready to ignite. Reaching her kitchen, she poured herself a steaming cup of coffee, lacing it with sweeteners from little pink packets. *"Mama liked her coffee black,"* Jodi remembered.

She then settled herself into the lushness of the overstuffed sofa in her living room. She faced the craggy flagstone fireplace, which was ablaze with a lustrous inferno. She began to read.

Susan,

How like her father, she thought not to use some sort of greeting. There was no, "Dear." Just, "Susan." No date, either.

"Saying that I am sorry is meaningless at this point," he continued. *"Dodo and I are happy together."*

"You are such an ass, dad. And who would ever name their daughter, Dodo? Jodi guessed that it was short for Dorothy or Doloras or maybe Doreen. She didn't know. She never asked.

"My reason for this letter is Michael. Your son is being totally obstinate and stubborn."

"Look at the pot calling the kettle black," she mused.

64

"Michael, has been invited by Dodo and me to spend Thanksgiving dinner with us. He won't because he feels that it would be hurtful to you. As always, Jodi has declined. Amy won't come either. This infuriates me. I want to spend the holidays with my kids."

Oh, my God! And your kids want to spend the holidays with their mother. They want to be in the only home they ever knew. They want to be there with Uncle Benny and Aunt Molly and Nonna Deligrossi. They want Nonna's special Italian wedding soup and Uncle Benny's famous clams casino, mom's traditional French cut green beans with almonds and fried onions and her Bourbon pecan smashed sweet potatoes and Aunt Molly's scrumptious homemade apple pies. They want to be a family. Not three kids sitting at a strange table staring at Dodo with no conversation, no laughing, no love.

"Now for the shocking part, Susan."

What could be more shocking than leaving her for Dodo? This should be good.

"Before you and I met, after my stint in Viet Nam, I was discharged from the navy. I decided to spend some time in San Diego. Being a part time handy man and beach bum was fun for awhile.

"I didn't know he did that." Jodi thought. He sure wasn't the beach bum type.

"I realized soon after I got there that my college girlfriend was living in the area. I got in touch with her and we got together. Well, to make a long story short, she got pregnant. I was there with her when she had a baby boy. She wanted to get married. I wasn't

interested. I had graduate school planned for the next semester at Cornell. My parents were furious about the whole thing. They met Karen once and were not impressed with her or with her family. I never did tell them that the baby was mine. We never discussed it. If they guessed, they never said anything to me. They were very persuasive in talking me into returning to New York. Karen was pushing me into marrying her. I left California. I never saw her again.

What a jerk! So, what about the baby, dad? What about him? Didn't you want to be a part of his life or help to raise him?

"Once back in New York, I met you. You were perfect. You were pretty and respectable. My parents loved you. We could live in Ithaca. You could teach. I could go to Cornell. So, the proposal, the wedding! I got Karen off my back for good. The rest is history."

"Oh, my God! He is telling her in a letter that he never really loved her. She was just a way out of a bad situation. What about Amy? Huh? What about that sweet little girl? Only love could create someone as special as she was. But, mom probably had enough love for the both of them."

What was the point in this letter, any way? Knowing that he never loved their mother was not going to get her to persuade his kids to go to his house to have Thanksgiving dinner with Dodo.

Jodi could not read any more. Her stomach felt upset. She was emotionally depleted. *"Poor mom! This letter must have rocked her with yet another enormous blow. It had to hit her like a one- two punch! But, she never let on. She was the strongest woman in the world."* Jodi wanted to tear the letter into a million pieces and throw it into the fireplace. Up in smoke! But, for some strange reason, she folded the letter, returned it to the envelope and popped it into the top drawer of her desk. Now Jodi was smiling as she remembered her mother. She wondered if her mother ever answered the letter.

Chapter Thirteen:

The Mystery Man, Unveiled

THE VERY NEXT DAY, SHE found RON's phone number. It was etched in her mother's address book under the Rs. She thought about calling. "No," she reconsidered. She would go there herself. She would meet him face to face. He was expecting her mother. But, Jodi would go in her mother's place and she would make clear to him why KIDs was not there.

Ron was nervous when he entered the restaurant. He was about fifteen minutes early. Wearing a brown suede jacket over a mint green V-neck sweater that showed off the blue of his eyes, he looked very handsome. His hair was a gorgeous silver color and he wore it short. His bangs were combed forward in a Caesar cut. He was mature looking, classy and sophisticated.

Checking his watch every few minutes, he became more and more troubled when it became apparent that his mystery woman might not show up. He remembered full well what his friends had said about cyber escapades. *"People who search for love on line must keep a grip on reality, have an open mind and not let unrealistic expectations surface."* He was cautioned time and again that on line dating was risky. But, this woman was different. She was genuine and sincere. She was also very sad. She told him about the loss of her child, a twelve year old girl who had battled a rare and dreadful congenital heart defect. He longed to meet her. Something very strong was pulling her towards him. After a half hour, he began to panic, ordering a Chevis Regal over ice to calm himself. They had both decided that it was best not to share real identities until after their first meeting.

He had no phone number to call. She did have his mobile phone number, though. He gave her his number without hesitation just in case she had to cancel. He didn't mind at all. He was a lot less worried about such things. He yanked his blackberry from his coat pocket to check for any missed calls. There were none. He set the phone on the table next to his plate to make sure not to miss a call.

There was one other set of diners in the room. Two men and two women were feasting on fried rice and chicken. He smiled as one of the ladies glanced in his direction and then went back to her buoyant conversation with the others. Their lighthearted laughter filled the room. The aroma of oil and lemon chicken came rushing towards him. He was ravenous. A pretty young Asian waitress came to his table for the third time. Again he told her that his dining partner would be arriving soon. He asked her to get him another drink. *"Make it a double, on the rocks, this time."*

Feeling awkward and a bit embarrassed, he was ready to call it a day, ask for the check and leave. Suddenly a very beautiful woman, holding a single red rose entered the restaurant. She looked shy and confused. *"This can't be her,"* he thought. *"She is too young to be my mystery woman."* Then the woman, spying him sitting there alone, nervously approached his table. "Hello," she said in a quivering wisp of a voice. *"I presume that you are Ron."* He looked intently at her in disbelief. She was lovely. Petite and angular, she had long chestnut hair and large blue eyes. She wore black slacks, a red Cornell sweatshirt under an open white quilted ski jacket. Under her arm, she carried a folded newspaper. This couldn't be his date. She was at least twenty years younger than what he had expected. *"What was going on?"* he wondered, not at all amused. She began by introducing herself as Jodi Phan.

Her story saddened him. It was such a tragedy for the young girl to have lost her mother in such a horrible accident. He fumbled for the right words,

Ill at ease, he sympathetically looked into her sad eyes, *"I am so sorry for your loss."*

"Thank you so much," she replied. Not knowing what else to say. This was a very uncomfortable moment for them both.

"I appreciate so much that you came here tonight," he said sympathetically.

"I had to come. My mother would have wanted me to. She would not have wanted you to think that she had intentionally ignored your dinner date." the girl responded sorrowfully, gazing briefly at him and then abruptly at the floor.

He replied politely, *"I am sure that it was difficult for you. It was obvious to me that your mother was a wonderful person. I enjoyed talking to her on the phone."*

Jodi ended the conversation. *"Yes, my mother was very special. She was so happy to be meeting you, as well. You would have loved her, I'm sure."* She was shocked at herself for saying, *"loved her"*. But, she wasn't sorry. Everyone loved her mother.

He graciously invited her to sit and join him for dinner.

Jodi respectfully refused his invitation. Her husband was waiting for her in the parking area outside of the restaurant. Tearfully, she gently embraced him. *"Thank you for befriending my mother, Ron,"* she whispered, as she placed the newspaper on the table. *"This is my mother's obituary."*

As she was walking away, he called to her. *"Take care of yourself. And by the way, R-O-N are my initials. My name is Rob O'Neil."* She did not look back. As Jodi left the restaurant, she had no idea who Rob O'Neil really was and he had no idea that she was the daughter of his long lost love.

His appetite gone, Rob sat back in his chair, motioned to the young Asian woman, who was watching him acutely, and asked her for the check, bearing in mind what a strange day it had been. Remembering the newspaper, he opened it to the obituary page.

As his eyes carefully perused the obituary page, he came to the memorial that her daughter had circled with a red marker.

Unable to let the truth sink in, he sat there for several minutes, gawking, paralyzed!

"Oh, my God," he gasped. What kind of an ill-fated hoax was played on him?

Sinking in his chair, feeling lightheaded and trembling wildly, he could not believe what he read. The name on the obituary was *"Susan Deligrossi Johnson."* It was his Susan.

Ithaca Daily News— *Susan Deligrossi Johnson,* a teacher at the Glasswing Residential Center, lost her life early Sunday morning in an automobile accident..

"Susan was the type of teacher who reached out to and connected well with students who were struggling in school. She let her students know she liked them and taught them discipline and self-respect. She was a bubbly Italian, full of vigor and spirit. The children all loved her because she created magic for them," said her friend, Christina Grover of Ithaca, "She was dynamic, very energetic and enthusiastic. You could tell she loved what she was doing and it was infectious. For Susan Johnson life was all about family, faith and friends. But probably more than anything else, it was about kids." "My mother was dedicated to children," said her son, Michael Johnson. "Our house was where all the neighborhood kids came to eat. There was sort of an open-door policy."

Benjamin Brown, Director of the Glasswing School, commented that "As far as a faculty member and teacher, she was one of the best. She looked for the best in in her students and really drove them to reach for that and to succeed to the point of their best work."

Ms. Johnson was raised in Cortland and graduated from Cortland High School and the Pennsylvania College of Education in East Bayfield City, Pennsylvania, where she received a degree in secondary education, majoring in English and Spanish. After raising her children, she went back to college to earn a master's *degree form Syracuse University and began teaching for the Office of Children and Family Services at the Glasswing facility.*

She is survived by her Mother, Josefina Deligrossi of Ithaca, her brother, Benjamin Deligrossi (Molly) of Buffalo, a son, Michael Johnson,(Rebecca) of Henderson, NV, a daughter, Jodi Phan (Seng) of Rochester, six grandchildren, Kaia Phan, Oliver Phan and Jenna Phan of Rochester and Mya, Alea and Makenna Marie Johnson of Henderson, NV. Ms. Johnson was predeceased by her father, "Bud", her brother, PFC Michael Deligrossi, killed in Viet Nam in 1968, and her beloved daughter Amy Johnson, who passed away at twelve years old in 1994.

A funeral mass and memorial service was held Wednesday at the Cathedral of the Immaculate Conception in Ithaca. Burial was in Rose Grove Catholic Memorial Park in Cortland.

In lieu of flowers, donations are being requested in Susan's memory for the Amy Johnson Perpetual Memorial Scholarship, given at the Ithaca High School every year. Please send donations to Stacey L. Lyntin, Box 237 Newfield, NY.

According to the obituary, she had a successful career. She was a teacher. Rob found that very fitting. He was saddened to read about the little girl that predeceased Susan. And Mike….he was shocked to see that Mike Deligrossi had been killed in Nam. He and Mike had played football together. Mike was a great guy.

His Susan was a grandmother! How could that be? None of it seemed real to him. For him, time had stood still and his beautiful Susan was still a teenage girl.

Secretly, Rob had always hoped that he and Susan some where, some time, some how would finish what they had started so many years before. After his failed marriage, he did try to find her. *"What an ironic turn of events,"* he thought unhappily, *"Susie and I came so close to getting together again. I guess it was just never meant to be. God, I loved her so much!"*

Rob tossed several bills on the table and left the restaurant, feeling very emotional. Driving slowly, on his way to his house, tears flowed liberally from his puffy, reddened eyes. He reminisced about their last day together. It was August 2, 1965. They were sitting on a blanket under the dazzling view of the cascading Buttermilk Falls, wrapped together in each other's arms, hungry for their love to burst out in passionate love making. He gave her a beautiful long stemmed red rose and she blushed. He told her that the rose symbolized his eternal love for her. He took her picture with his instant camera and they chuckled as it was released. She looked so beautiful sitting there, in the midst of the scenic beauty of the waterfalls. It was a "bitter sweet" day, knowing full well that their time together was limited. Why?

He wondered why he had let his parents and hers so cruelly break them up. They were young, too young to realize the consequences of letting go. She was his first love and he never, ever felt about anyone else the way he did about her. He kept track of her for several years. After hearing that she married, he freed her from his mind, trying hard to accept life without her in it.

The day after he met Jodi in the restaurant, he visited the cemetery. There she was cuddled up between a score of other Deligrossis and a little girl, named Amy. He promised her that he would visit her often. And, he did.

Chapter Fourteen:

It Can't be True!

SEVERAL MONTHS LATER, JODI WAS getting ready go to the market when the phone rang. "Hello," she answered it on the second ring. "Yes, this is Jodi Phan."

"Hello, Mrs. Phan. This is Sgt. Paul Trent of the Tompkins County Sheriff's Department. I have been assigned to investigate the accident that took Susan Johnson's life earlier this year. I am sorry for your loss."

"Oh, yes. Hello, Sgt. Trent. I remember you from the initial investigation." Her heart was pounding. Her hands were trembling.

"It has come to our attention that the brakes on your mother's car may have been tampered with. The wrecker service that towed the car the night of the accident recently had it inspected by a local mechanic and he became aware of the brake problem. With no working brakes, she was doomed on those snow covered roads. We

found cut brake lines and lug nuts that had been slightly loosened on the front and rear of the car. "

"Oh, my God." Now her voice was quivering along with her hands. *"How? Why? It doesn't make any sense. No one would want to hurt my mother."*

"Well," he whispered, *" It looks like some one did want to hurt her. And since she is dead, it looks to me like manslaughter, if not premeditated murder."*

"That is ridiculous," Jodi screeched. *"Every one loved my mom."* Now, her head hurt and she felt faint.

"I need you to come to my office as soon as possible so that we can iron out some things." now he was severe and forceful.

"I will," she replied in a very apprehensive, nervous voice. *" I will be there today."*

When she hung up the receiver, she had to sit for a minute to steady her shaking legs. She settled herself onto one of the deep, leather recliners that faced the massive fireplace in her spacious living room. She was confused, angry and filled with emotion. She had to think. *"How could this be? Who could it be? No, it couldn't be."*

Jodi called her brother, Mike, and he was just as mystified by the turn in events as she was. She also phoned her Uncle Benny, her mother's brother, who was a prominent attorney in an adjoining state. They spoke for several minutes. Benny Deligrossi was confused and bewildered. Jodi promised her brother and her uncle that she would keep both up to date after her visit with the sheriff.

She tore off her jeans and Maui t-shirt, slipped off her Nikes and opted for a more suitable pair of black dress slacks, a white pinstriped blouse with a button down collar and black chunky sandals. She threw a soft yellow cardigan sweater over her shoulders. Her hair was in a ponytail, tied at the nape of her neck. She pulled out the rubber band that held it together and pulled a brush threw the golden brown curls before grabbing her purse, car keys and sunglasses.

The Tompkins County Sheriff's Office was nestled between a string of large pine trees on Route 13 between Ithaca and Cortland, NY. Jodi parked the car in the only available spot in the lot. She power locked the doors and entered the building to be greeted by the secretary, a small middle aged woman with horn rimmed glasses and an outdated hair do. She showed Jodi to Sgt. Trent's office.

Trent was not at all what she expected. He looked more like a doctor or clergyman than a police officer. He was slight, wide eyed and clean shaven. His smile showed off a set of dazzling white teeth and his demeanor was poised and sophisticated.

After showing Jodi to a high backed wooden chair at the other side of his desk, he posed a ton of questions. Some she couldn't answer. He wanted to know why her mother was driving any where at that hour with those road conditions. Leaning forward in his chair, he smiled sympathetically, as he listened. Piecing information together that she had from a note that her mother had taped to the door, she knew that her mother had been summoned to Glasswing. Her mother was expecting a friend to pick her up in the morning for church. That's why the note was there. Her mother scribbled out a quick message stating that one of the students was having a melt down. Trent sat back in his chair, sighing. She was supposedly the only one that the boy trusted. Someone from Glasswing called her to see if she could lend them a hand in trying to calm him down. But, clearly, she never got there. The note was found the next day by the woman who was supposed to be driving Susan to church. That is all that Jodi knew. It wasn't unusual for her mother to do something above and beyond her contractual hours to help a kid in need.

"Hmm," Sgt. Trent *was very deep in thought. "I guess we need to talk to some people at her work. It is very strange to me that they would call her in during those weather conditions. Very irresponsible and inconsiderate."* He paused for a moment to clear his throat. "I remember that day." He began fidgeting with his pen, doodling incoherent lines on the back of a sheet of yellow lined paper. *"Yep,"* he thought, *" I was on duty that night. There were hundreds of ice storm victims hunkered down in frigid homes and shelters in the north country. I remember that they were expecting at least a week without power. People were waiting in long lines to buy generators, firewood, groceries and bottled water. Not much better here in this county. It was a bad one."*

Jodi also remembered that day. The snow, the beauty! All of a sudden it had turned on her. It became a perilous enemy.

"My mother was a very cautious driver. She would never drive heedlessly under any conditions," Jodi responded uneasily.

"With the way that her car had been altered and the condition of the roads that night, it wouldn't matter how safely she drove. She was doomed." the sergeant informed her understandingly.

80

Jodi stood up and eased herself toward the door. Trent was aware of her edginess. She was ready to leave. He understood.

"We will get to the bottom of this, Mrs. Phan." the sergeant assured her with confidence as he walked her to her car.

"Drive carefully and thank you for seeing me," he said, opening her car door for her, *"I will keep you informed."* Jodi drove off, bearing the weight of the world on her cardigan covered shoulders.

As she drove off, Trent thought to himself, *"Nice girl. Too bad."*

Chapter Fifteen:

Revenge, a Confession of Pain

JESUS VISITED HIS SISTER'S GRAVE faithfully every Sunday morning, bathing the white slab marker with dahlias, red roses, chrysanthemums, and yellow lilies.

He examined the gravestone that simply read, "Manuela Maria Garcia de Moreno." He wanted to snatch her from her casket and hold her closely one more time underneath the safety of the old faded quilt.

He had made his plans. He had contacted Chico Alverez. He had negotiated a deal and because of the magnitude of what he was asking Chico to do, the price tag would be plenty. In fact, this could be Chico's last job. Jesus was giving him enough money to retire on. Chico was getting $25,000 for each hit. With the four hits that was a nice piece of change.

The whole transaction was complex and dangerous. Chico was delving into arenas where he had never been before. He dickered back and forth with Jesus for quite some time to discuss the specifics. No, this was not going to be easy. Chico was not at all eager for all of this to go down. He felt like Jesus was turning into a mad man and everything was getting out of control. Chico deduced that Jesus was paranoid, pathological and very, very dangerous.

The men conducted their business in the back room of the pawn shop, which was one of Jesus's business enterprises. Chico was the first to talk.

"OK, Jesus. What's the deal? ¿Qué tipo de trabajo loco tiene para mí esta vez?

"Buddy Cruz is first on the hit list. You and I will take him out together. Then you do Reed in and make it hurt. Susan Johnson is all yours. Make hers look like an accident."

"After that, we'll get some one on the inside at Walton to put the squeeze on Jimmy Dentes. Lenny Turango is a good bet. We can lean on him with no trouble. He's got a kid in Queens. Cute little thing. She lives with Lenny's sister-in-law. That kid is everything to him. All we have to do is throw his little girl's name around and he'll be putty in our hands. He'll do anything for us."

Lenny Turango was a bear of a man. His giant physique was a threat to anyone who got in his way. For a long while, things were going pretty well for him. He had a decent job as a doorman in a swanky Madison Avenue hotel. Robust tips kept him pretty well off. He had a wife that he loved and a baby daughter that he adored. Without forewarning, the floor ripped out from under him and his world stopped. When he caught his wife with another guy in his own apartment, he used his brute force to tear the man apart. The poor guy ended up in the hospital for a month. Lenny ended up at

Walton. Soon afterwards, Lenny's wife died. It was cancer. His little girl went to live with her aunt.

Chico didn't like anything about the job. Everything about it bothered him. But, his greed overpowered his commonsense.

"Creo que estoy tratando con un loco loco. Creo que estoy tratando con un loco loco. Esta idea me ha rastreo con pesar."

Carlos contemplated. He always began thinking in Spanish when he was troubled or annoyed.

He was sure that Jesus was insane. Remembering the first job that he did for Jesus, made him break out into a nervous sweat. After butchering the poor soul, he ripped a sterling silver St. Christopher medal from the old stiff's neck. It was oval shaped with the inscription, "St. Christopher Be My Guide." Chico also snatched a leather wallet from the guy's pant's pocket. There were exactly three tens, two fives and four ones in the wallet. There was also a driver's license. It was a class C. *"Son of a bitch was a trucker,"* he snarled. *"What the hell kind of beef did Jesus have with a hauler? The guy was probably one of Jesus's bagboys, delivering from the factory to the hood. Some how he must have bilked on a transaction."* Later on, Chico tossed the naked body into the Hudson.

Chapter Sixteen:

Not From Here

SGT. TRENT AND A DETECTIVE from the sheriff's department stood in front of the gate at the Glasswing Residential Detention Center. The detective, Terry Grant, was a thick-necked, brown skinned, former high school offensive guard. He was Trent's protégé. Trent rescued him from the streets of Syracuse when he was just a kid, raised him and sent him to college, where Grant got a degree in criminal justice. Grant was like a son to Trent and the older man wanted him on this assignment. Grant had a hell of a nose for smelling out a rat.

Glasswing was located on a major highway, which connected Ithaca, NY to Elmira, NY. It was a large secure facility that housed youthful offenders. It housed boys primarily from large cities, like Rochester, Syracuse, Buffalo, Utica and the boroughs of New York City. Most of them were black. There were also some Latinos, but very few white kids. Trent's voice tightened as he looked in Grant's direction, *"I wonder if the white dudes in trouble were just lucky enough to hire better attorneys."* Grant smiled faintly and shrugged his shoulders, thankful that he had escaped the hood.

The facility opened in 1977 and was located adjacent to the Brentwood Correctional Detention Center, which incarcerated teenage girls. Both centers provided residential care for a capacity of fifty to sixty youthful offenders. Intensive supervision and services were provided by a staff of resident advisors, case management specialist, psychologists, teachers, nurses, and support staff. Residents at both places received five hours of academic instruction five days a week and participated in life skills groups, and recreational and leisure activities. Bulky razor wire barriers enclosed the boundaries of each facility. The two sites created an ominous and murky picture for any one driving past them.

From the gate, Trent and Greene were able to see a young man walking slowly in front of one of the guards, who had bulging biceps that dominated his tight fitting uniform. The boy and the guard were getting into to a state van parked in the large lot to the left of the building. Another guard sat in the driver's seat of the van, waiting for the duo to enter the caged rear area. The boy, who wore a bright yellow jumpsuit, was hand cuffed and shackled. He faced the ground, shoulders hunched as he walked awkwardly with the cumbersome restraints hampering his every step. Sgt. Trent assumed that the boy was on his way to either court or to a doctor's appointment.

Sgt. Trent pressed the button on the intercom at the gate to alert the staff that they were there. After a few seconds, a severe sounding voice answered back.

"How can I help you?"

"We have an appointment to see your director, Ben Brown. We are from the sheriff's department." Trent retorted forcefully.

"Hold on," the voice echoed.

The clanging thud of the gate startled the two men. They walked through one, then two, then three more gates before they arrived at a metal detector. At long last, taking off their watches, and putting coins, cell phones, and car keys into a wire bin, they were able to enter the large reception center. A bulky uniformed employee, who was strapped up, gave them a form to sign and then signaled them to yet one more door.

The two men entered an office area, passing several young women, who were typing energetically on keyboard pads. Several of the women smiled briskly as the two men passed. Trent and Grant eventually came to the end of a very long passageway and rapped on a door that had Ben Brown's name engraved in silver letters. "Benjamin S. Brown, Rehabilitation Director."

Ben Brown opened the door, shook hands with the two men and directed them to two black leather chairs that fit neatly into a large conference table.

Brown looked much younger than his fifty years. He was tall, lean and good looking. His hair was a dark chestnut, receding at the top. His face was suntanned. Wearing casual, expensive clothes, he looked relaxed, as if he had just stepped off a cruise ship returning from some exotic location. *"Thanks for seeing us,"* Trent said.

The two police officers parked themselves in the chairs. Trent, sighed as he submerged his exhausted body into the plush of the soft leather.

"My pleasure," responded Brown. *"Susan Johnson was a wonderful teacher. She passed through an inspiring life's journey. We all miss her. Whatever I can do, I will do."*

"We need to know who called her the night of her accident. Who would ask her to drive in those conditions and for what reason?" This time Grant did the talking.

"That is what has had me concerned, too," Brown cried out. *"No one would. They would have to call me in order to make any outside calls in the middle of the night. We do not have an officer on duty at those hours to give the ok. I am the only one who can endorse any over night calls."*

"And did you?" Trent asked.

"No, of course not." Brown came back with quickly. *"that would be unreasonable to call a teacher in at that hour to off set a melt down. That is what our guards do, not our teachers. Moreover, there were no problems with any of our inmates that night. I checked all of the log books for every unit in this building. Nothing unusual at all. Our video cameras were all activated and no one at all used any of our phones at that hour.'*

"How about a mobile phone?" Grant retorted forcibly.

"No cell phones are allowed in the program areas. We can't take a chance that a kid could get hold of one. Of course, our people have been known to slip contraband items in before. It can happen," Brown replied.

"So in your professional opinion, that call was not made from here that night." Trent inquired brusquely.

"Not from here," Brown repeated, *"Not from here."*

After thanking Ben Brown for his cooperation, Trent and his detective left the facility. They both agreed that the person who called Susan Johnson the night she died did not do it from Glasswing. Trent was impatient to get her phone records. He requested them from the phone company and expected them to be on his desk in the morning.

Chapter Seventeen:

Shark Bait, for Sure

SASSY MCQUEEN WAS A TOUGH hoodrat from the most shady part of the Bronx. She was at Brookwood for grand larceny and she had been locked up before for several drug charges, selling and using. She was nearly seventeen years old, with just a year to spare before they stuck her in an adult penitentiary. She knew how to play the system and she could con the boots off a cowboy.

Sassy was a scrawny, black girl with unruly dreadlocks. There was no doubt that she was one mean, nasty, homely wench. Her street wise attitude did not curry favor with the adults at Brentwood. Besides being sneaky and underhanded, Sassy was practically illiterate. She never went to school long enough to learn to read fluently or write well. It was challenging for her to decipher the simplest words. She had a short fuse and unlike most girls in detention, she didn't internalize problems. Sassy was more like the boys at Glasswing, who would act out through yelling or hitting.

She had no close friends outside of lock up. The only people she rolled with were other felons that she met inside Brentwood.

Sassy had given birth to baby daughter the year before. She screamed and hollered the little girl out of her belly and into the world. After its birth, she only took a momentary glimpse at the infant. All she could see was a mop of dark black hair, still wet from birthing. A nurse came to get the baby right from the delivery room to prepare the child for adoption. Sassy had heard the doctors say something about it having an addiction to drugs. They sent the baby off in a small incubator with the nurse. Sassy didn't care much. She never thought about that baby again.

Sassy hated her cottage mate. Manuela Moreno was everyone's poster child. She could do no wrong at Brentwood. The girls had nothing in common and Manuela was terrified of Sassy's violent outbursts and tetchiness. She pleaded with the staff to be reassigned to another room and eventually, her request was approved. That really incensed Sassy. No one ever got that kind of preferential treatment at Brentwood. Besides, Manuela made Sassy look like a scrub and Sassy was not going to let her get away with that.

Sassy knew that Manuela was one of Darren Reed's girls. She was going to keep her ear to the wall. Darren would appreciate any information that she could give him about his little Spanish Prima Donna. But, even more than she despised Manuela, Sassy hated Miss Johnson, that Pollyanna, goodie goodie, who couldn't mind her own friggin' business.

One afternoon, as she was leaving work, Susan Johnson got a call from one of the social workers at Brentwood, Glasswing's sister school. It was Ellyn Carlson, a dedicated, hard- working woman, who needed a favor from Susan.

"Hello, Ellyn" Susan answered cheerfully. *"What's up?"*

After some polite conversation, Ellyn proceeded to tell Susan what she had on her mind.

"I have this girl here at Brentwood who really doesn't belong here. She is a good kid who fell into bad circumstances. We do not have the personnel here to give her additional tutoring so that she can catch up with her classmates back home. She has a great scholarship to a good catholic school and we want to be able to keep it for her. The judge was a callous son of a bitch who gave her a year here with no "good behavior" clause. Do you have some time to come over here to work with her? It will only take a day or two a week. She is a smart kid and eager to learn." Ellyn went on and on.

Susan, who had a difficult time saying *"no"* to anyone who needed her help, agreed. *"Sure,"* she said willingly, *"I think that I can manage that. I will stop by there tomorrow afternoon and meet the girl. We will see how things go from there."*

Ellyn was grateful, *"You are an angel, Susan. Thanks so much. The girl's name is Manuela. Manuela Moreno."*

Susan began working with Manuela the next evening. Ellyn was right. Manuela was a delight to work with. She was an eager, enthusiastic learner and she put in an enormous amount of effort. She had goals and willpower. She was totally remorseful and apologetic for her past behavior and she wanted desperately to make amends to her family and to society. Manuela was so ashamed of her past choices. The young girl and her tutor bonded instantly. Susan saw a sweet gentleness in Manuela and Manuela embraced and absorbed all of Susan's nurturing, encouragement and love. They became friends and confidants.

Manuela began to share everything with Susan. She had a compelling story to tell. Manuela talked about her mother and her brother and their life in el barrio. And, she talked about Julia. That is when the insightful teacher first became aware of the overwhelming pain that had taken over the young girl.

After several weeks, Manuela began to talk to Susan about things that made her happy, things that she missed. She told Susan about life in el barrio. She became excited talking about how she loved to explore the district hub on East 116th Street, where she could stroll along Jefferson Park. She chatted breathlessly about how much she loved to head down to El Museo Del Barrio on Fifth Avenue's *"Museum Mile"* or up to the colorful Keith Haring mural on the riverside. She was animated telling Susan all about the wonderful oozing slices of Manhattan pizza at the world famous *Patsy's.*

Manuela gave Susan a mini lesson about the celebrations in her neighborhood, such as El Dia de las Candelarias. It was held every year on the eve of February 2nd and her people built huge bonfires around which they danced and drank and chanted, *"Viva las candelerias."* She babbled on and on about the mouth watering foods that her mother prepared for them and how her brother would keep the salsa music going late into the night. Susan was fascinated to learn how the Puerto Ricans celebrated most Christian holidays, including Christmas and Easter, as well as New Year's Day. In addition, Manuela's family, celebrated "Three King's Day," each

January 6. It was on this day, Manuela's favorite, that Puerto Rican children looked forward to gifts, which are said to be delivered by "the three wise men." On the days leading up to January 6, Puerto Ricans had continuous celebrations. Parrandiendo is a practice similar to American and English caroling, in which neighbors went visiting house to house. Other major celebration days were The Day of the Race—Columbus Day and St. James Day. Every June, Puerto Ricans in New York and other large cities celebrated Puerto Rican Day. Manuela loved the parades held on that day, which have come to rival St. Patrick's Day parades and celebrations in popularity.

"That sounds like such wonderful fun." Susan wanted to share her own traditions with Manuela. *"I grew up in a similar neighborhood, where the Italian immigrants celebrated their heritage. We had a wonderful feast day for St. Rocco, a patron saint of the Italians. It was festive and the Italian feasts that were presented were unbelievably delicious."*

Manuela was intrigued.

Susan added. *"There were traditional Italian gastronomic delights, such as limoncello to take home, or a feast to enjoy then and there. They had all of my favorite Italian dishes: pizza fritta, tiramisu, gnocchi, braciole, polenta, and chicken riggies with red cherry peppers."*

All of a sudden, Manuela was starving.

"One year, when I was a junior in high school, I was actually chosen to be Miss Italian American. It was quite a privilege. I remember that my dad was very proud of me. I got to wear a beautiful white dress and a crown and I carried red roses. In

church, at a special mass, I left the roses at the foot of a statue of the Virgin Mother." Susan blushed as she went on about that special honor.

And, Manuela told Susan all about the seedy Darren Reed.

Susan was so afraid that Darren Reed would stalk and pester Manuela when she returned home. What she had heard about the street hustler turned her stomach. She couldn't comprehend that horrible world of insalubrious people that Manuela was doomed to return to.

Jesus never realized that Susan Johnson was striving to help his little sister. The more that Susan did on Manuela's behalf, the more Sassy McQueen detested them both. Susan was guarded when it came to Sassy and she ignored her as much as possible.

One day, in the dining hall, Sassy deliberately tripped Manuela as she was carrying her food tray to the table. Losing her footing, Manuela's mashed potatoes, gravy, fried chicken, peas, milk and peaches spilled to the floor, spattering all over her red and yellow jumpsuit.

"You is pretty ham-fisted there, Manny Girl," Sassy hissed, followed by a thunderous clamor of clapping and laughing from other girls at Sassy's table. Manuela gave Sassy a dirty look and flipped her off.

Sassy came back with, *" Now why you gotta jump off like that, ho. You actin' just like one uh those thugs from the crib. What 'sup with you, any way throwing F-bombs at me like that?"* Ending her verbal abuse, Sassy replied angrily with, *"Peace out, bitch!"*

Sassy felt triumphant as Manuela stooped to the floor to pick up the food strewn across the room. When another girl tried to help

Manuela, Sassy kicked the girl hard in the shin and bellowed, *"Let the scrub handle her own mess."*

"Now, I am shark bait for sure," Manuela whimpered to herself.

That night Manuela cried herself to sleep. When she woke up the next morning, the sun tiptoed through the small window of her room, giving her hope.

Chapter Eighteen:

Memories Embroidered on My Soul

SOON AFTER HER MOTHER'S MEMORIAL service, Susan's dearest friend, Jayne Marshall, flew in from Seattle to spend some time with Jodi and her family. Jayne most likely knew Jodi's mother better than anyone else in the world. They had been friends for years, since college. Jayne had eased Susan through a lot of challenging situations. Even though the two women were separated by a vast expanse of the country, Susan could always lean on Jayne. Susan considered Jayne to be the sister that she never had. They depended on one another when things got complicated in their lives.

Jayne was clearly still shaken at the sudden loss her best friend. She tried very hard to stay composed and stoic for Jodi's sake, but it was not an easy thing to do. One evening, after Jodi put her three children to bed and her husband, a physician, was on call at the hospital, the two women were left alone to appreciate some quiet time together and to relish in some remembering. Escaping to the living room, they sat on a braided carpet in front of the Phan's immense fireplace. Mr. Bojangles rested between them, snuggling up to Jodi

Jayne pulled her legs beneath her and Jodi sprawled out the length of the hearth rug, her long legs very nearly reaching the soothing flames of the fire. Jodi had chilled two bottles of red wine and set them on a serving dish. She had prepared a plate of hummus, pita chips, slices of exotic cheeses, green grapes, and hunks of summer sausage with honey mustard on the side. They shed tears, cuddling and consoling one another until the first bottle of wine was consumed. Popping the second cork, the two women began to talk about Susan.

Jayne reminded Jodi about the time that her mother had gone to the hospital for a mammogram and had no idea how to put on the three holed hospital gown. She did not see any instructions in the dressing room, so she was condemned to figure it out for herself. Susan reasoned that in view of the fact that she was having her breasts examined, clearly one hole was for one arm, one hole was for the other arm and the third hole was obviously for a boob. That made perfect sense to Susan. Who would ever think that you had to put one arm through a hole, wrap the entire garment around and put the other arm in another hole and then drape it across your body so the first arm goes into the same hole again. Poor Susan went into the "women only" waiting room with a boob hanging out of a hole. Other women in the room were snickering, hardly able to hold back rolls of laughter. Finally, a "laughing so hard she could pee" RN came to her rescue. *No, no, Mrs. Johnson! Let me help you with the gown!"* Jodi roared at the thought of it.

Susan, of course was duly mortified. All she could think of was that someone in the room would recognize her in church!

Can't you just see mom sitting in the waiting room, reading *Better Homes and Gardens* with her boob hanging there for the world to see?" Jodi howled, hysterically. *"It was good to laugh,"* she thought.

Susan, herself would tell that story over and over again, amusing so many people. That was the funny Susan. The one who could laugh at herself and see the comedy in every situation.

They also evoked memories of the tender, caring Susan. They talked about how she had befriended a homeless man in the Bronx when Amy was a patient at Columbia Presbyterian. At first, she had shunned him. But, Amy was sad about that and asked her mom to be nice to the scruffy, unkempt stranger, who had taken residence on the steps of the hospital. Paying attention to her sick child's wishes, she did just that. She would take a seat on the steps next to the man and visit with him whenever she needed a retreat from the morose venue of the intensive care's pediatric wing. After Amy's death, that man was there to support Susan in her darkest hours. They were as different as mice and monkeys, but he was there for the brokenhearted mother whose life had just been worn to shreds forever. He listened. He consoled. He understood! He was like an angel sent from heaven. Susan was so grateful for him. She knew that Amy had somehow known how much her mother had needed someone. It was fate! It was destiny!

Jodi remembers how scared she was for her mother when she had to fend for herself on the streets of New York City.

Then Jodi began to ask questions. Lots and lots of questions!

"What do you remember about my mother?"

"Oh, my God!!! Where do I start? So many things pop into my mind. Let's see. She loved pizza with anchovies and jalapenos."

"Yuck!!! I know. Jodi interrupted. Giggling.

"Tank tops and jeans were her favorite attire. But, she had impeccable style when she had to go out. She was a sun worshiper and loved camping and hiking. She preferred wine to beer. But, Susan loved any kind of drink that came in a cocktail glass with a cute little umbrella."

More giggles from Jodi.

"She could not come to my way of thinking about eating meat."

Jodi remembered that Jayne was a staunch vegetarian. Her mother used to lovingly call her best friend a "tree hugging, granola bar."

"She loved steaks and hamburgers, rare. She was a political junky and the Kennedy brothers were her idols. She cheered unfalteringly for the New York Yankees and the Buffalo Bills. She was so proud of all of the useless trivia that she had in her head. She could name all of the townships in Cortland County and list all of the names of Henry the Eighth's wives. Like, who really cares?

Jodi nodded in agreement, smiling.

She had a hell of a golf swing, but her short game needed work. She was pretty pathetic on the greens."

"So true," thought Jodi. Her mom could get to the green in two shots and have a five putt on a Par Four.

"*And Don Mattingly,*" Jodi blurted out excitedly. "*Mom that that south paw was the greatest ballplayer ever.*"

Now Jayne is smiling. She knew what Susie thought. "*He sure does look hot in baseball pants,*" Jayne remembers her friend commenting with a twinkle in her eye.

"*She read Moby-Dick by Herman Melville, Brothers Karamazov by Fyodor Dostoevsky, War and Peace by Leo Tolstoy, Don Quixote by Miguel de Cervantes, Great Expectations by Charles Dickens and Jane Eyre by Charlotte Brontë more then once.*"

Yes. Jodi remembers that her mom was the only mom at the beach immersed in the classics. All the others were reading Danielle Steele.

"*She loved all kinds of music from country to classical, from George Straight to Francesco Cavalli. Andrew Wyeth was her favorite artist and she never, ever wore purple and red together. She laughed about never, ever being able to be a Red Hatter.*"

More chuckles.

"*She was a great cook. Her zuppa inglesa was first-rate.*"

"*That was my great- grandmother's recipe,*" Jodi remembered. "*The one who died at child birth. It was handed down to my mother.*"

Zuppa inglesa was a rich and delicious family favorite. Susan made it for special occasions, especially for baptisms and other religious get-togethers. The dessert was a classic Italian trifle made with custard and chocolate layered with liqueur-soaked cake, most commonly rum.

"She loved to travel and her dream was to stay one night at the Hotel del Coronado in San Diego. I never could figure that one out," Jayne continued.

Jodi remembers her mom telling her that years before she had seen a travel documentary about the hotel. She always wanted to see it for herself. She never did.

"Did my mom date anyone before she met my dad?'

"Of course, she did. She was a beautiful girl. She had a lot of dates."

"Was there any one special, before dad?"

"Yes, very special. She broke up with someone that she cared deeply about. It was way before I met her. They were high school sweethearts."

"No kidding! I didn't know that. What happened to him?"

"Don't know. Susie didn't share much of that with me. I just know that she was very sad for a long time. She even detached herself from her family for awhile. She got a job as a waitress at college and kind of sheltered herself in her education. She didn't go home to visit a lot. She just worked and studied."

"I can't even imagine that. She and Nonna have always been so close."

Jodi sighed deeply as Jayne went on. Mr. Bojangles, sensing the uneasiness in the room, put his paw on Jodi's knee. She, in turn, gently stroked the sheen of his silky coat.

"I don't know what part her family took in the break-up, Jodi. I don't even remember his name. Funny. She must have mentioned his name a hundred times and it's gone. I can't recall it. I am not sure why she isolated herself from her family. I do know that

he was very handsome and athletic, a football star. She kept a scrapbook at college with news articles about his prowess on the football field. He went off to some ivy league college. I know that one day, out of the blue, she tossed the scrapbook in the trash bin. Just like that. I asked her why. She just shrugged her shoulders and said that eventually we have to get over things. She had kind of an epiphany, I guess. She had a strong, vibrant recovery. Came back to the world, you might say. What ever happened to her and the boy from her past wounded her intensely. But, she met your dad and got married and became the best mother in the whole world."

"She sure did." Jodi smiled at Jayne after giving the other woman a huge hug.

"I do know that your mom was very proud of you and Michael. She was also pleased with your spouses. She marveled at Seng and how he left for the United States with his family when he was little. She often talked to me about how they traveled in that small boat from Laos and how he worked so hard to learn the English language and get his education. And....the babies! She loved those little grandbabies of hers so much."

"I know she did." Now, Jodi was struggling to keep back the tears.

"Did you know my Uncle Mikey?" Jodi had heard so much about him throughout the years.

"Heavens, yes! I met him when he was home from boot camp. He came to see your mom in Pennsylvania. I think it was our sophomore year in college. Mikey was drop dead gorgeous. He was the epitome of tall, dark and handsome, very muscular with

chiseled good looks. He was really nice, too. He wanted to be a commercial pilot when he got out of the military. He was due to be discharged a few months after he was killed in Nam. It was terrible! Susan was numb with grief and your grandfather never got over Mikey's death. His hair turned snow white over night and his heart failed. He had to sell his barber shop and he lost his will to live."

Jodi listened attentively. Mr. Bojangles wagged his tail rapidly and placed his head at Jodi's feet.

"That is about the time that Susie reconnected with her family. Actually, it's about the time that she threw that scrapbook away. I never really put two and two together before. I think it was Mikey's death that turned everything around. Your Uncle Benny had a real hard time with it, too. At the time, Benny was in college. He was a fervent anti- war protester, a real long-haired, flag burning liberal."

"Uncle Benny! My Uncle Benny! My very conservative, conventional Uncle Benny. Gosh! Time sure changes people!" Jodi squealed in disbelief.

"No honey, circumstances change people. He and Mikey had been fighting two different battles. Mikey lost his battle and when Mikey died, Benny gave up on his. Years later Benny and your Aunt Molly went to the Viet Nam Memorial. Finding Mikey's name there, was the beginning of the healing process for him. He went to Washington DC to mourn, to remember, to reflect on war and on death, and to heal. It was a powerfully cathartic moment for him. He was overwhelmed with pride for all of the servicemen who

had lost their lives in that very controversial war that changed our world forever."

"Growing up in the sixties must have been exciting!" Jodi assumed.

"Being a kid in the sixties was exciting and difficult, all in one. With the Beatles, Bob Dylan, and the Rolling Stones, an alternative music culture became a dominant force. Civil rights protest rallies set forth peaceful demonstrations. There was a sexual revolution, birth control pills, a moonwalk and Woodstock. There were the dance crazes, like the twist, the mashed potato, the watusi and the hully gully. That was the exciting part. On the other hand, we had the assassinations of a very popular president and the charismatic Dr. King. The war, itself, profoundly changed our country. It shattered our national honor and pride and made a whole generation question our government. We were overcome with change."

Overcome, herself, Jodi changed the subject to her father.

"Do you think that mom hated my dad?" Jodi always wondered, never having the nerve to ask. "After he left her."

Jodi thought carefully before answering.

"I know that she didn't hate him at all. I think that Sean thinks that she did, though. In fact, she prayed that he would go back to her. She begged God to sent him back. If he had, she would be right there; ready to forgive and forget and to get on with it. She hated being divorced. I always told her to beware of what she prayed for."

"And, what about Dodo?" Jodi persisted.

"Oh, no doubt, she did resent Dodo a lot. She heard from several people from the insurance agency that Dodo had her eyes on your dad for years. Dodo had made reference of that to several co-workers. She was very flirty with him, seduced him pretty much. Your mom understood that it takes two to tango, but she could never forgive Dodo for taking your dad away from all of you. That is exactly how she saw it, that Dodo "took him" away. After all, Dodo knew he was married and that he had three small children and a sick little girl, to boot. Your mom had very strong values. That ole' parochial school catechism kicked in a lot with her. If something was wrong, in her mind, she couldn't validate it. She couldn't let go. She held true to her moral code."

Jayne was about to admit something to Jodi that she hadn't told anyone, except Susan.

"In fact, for awhile I was seeing a married man. It was short lived and I am not proud of it. He was an old friend who I reconnected with through the internet's Classmates. COM. Your mom told me in no uncertain terms what she thought about that. It shocked her and she was disappointed in me. The guy's wife found out and the affair ended. That period in my life was an emotional roller coaster ride from hell. I knew that your mom was quick to judge because of what had happened to her. But, Susie felt sorry for the wife and she was scared for me. Guess, that makes sense. I was grateful that she cared enough to tell me how she felt. Your mom didn't hold it against me, or anything. She and I got through it."

"Are you dating, now?" Jodi was so hoping that Jayne was content with her life.

Jayne laughed nervously before answering. *"I am. He is a sports photographer from Tacoma. He travels all over the world."*

Jodi noticed how Jayne began to brighten up when she began talking about her guy.

"He is in Augusta right now, where he is shooting the Master's tournament. He is following Tiger Woods around all day. Not a bad way to earn a buck. He is a bit avant-garde. He and I are a lot alike. Oh, and by the way, he is a vegan. I'm not sure if he's a "keeper" because he gets me press passes to all the golf tourneys or if it's because he's a vegan. It's not easy to find a vegan who is my age. Most men have to have their prime rib on a daily basis."

Jayne gives out a hearty laugh.

"Any thing else you want to know, my dear?"

"Wedding bells?" Jodi interjected shyly.

"Hell no! I am not the marrying kind. I like my independence too much. Too set in my ways. Besides, he has been married three times. The first wife gets half his retirement. The second one stuck him with alimony. The third one lasted all of ten minutes. He's pretty gun shy. I like it that way. Any more questions, Missy?'

Jayne was ready for anything.

Jodi sat up suddenly. She told Jayne that she had something that she wanted to share with her. She quietly walked over to her desk. Mr, Bojangles stirred, got up and followed Jodi. Underneath a cluster of papers, she located an envelope. Walking back to her spot on the carpet, she offered it to Jayne.

"Did my mother ever tell you about this letter?"

Reading it over twice and examining it pensively, Jayne flinched a few times and shook her head in disbelief.

"No, never. She never mentioned this letter to me. This puts a totally different light on things. I always believed that tragedy could bring a couple closer together or tear them apart. Amy's illness consumed your mother. She used to feed Amy with a medicine dropper every hour so that the baby would get enough nutrition. Her little body didn't have the strength to suck from a bottle. And the medications that Amy was on were mind boggling. There were so many of them. Susan used to worry so about giving Amy the wrong meds at the wrong time. Susan would go into panic mode whenever a virus was going around, For Amy, a common cold or flu could be life threatening."

Jodi put her head down, fixing her eyes on the floor as she remembered. The dutiful lab sat in constant devotion, watching over her lovingly, as if he could feel her every emotion.

"It took its toll on her. She was exhausted much of the time. I wondered if the wall of pain that she built around herself began to shut Sean out. Your dad was always a career oriented workaholic. He wasn't very forthright with his emotions. Your mom and dad were so different in the way they dealt with Amy's illness. Susan faced it head on and Sean pretended that it never happened."

Jodi shook her head in recognition.

"I assumed that their grief over Amy had created a growing gulf between them. But, no, I gave him too much credit. What he did by sending this letter was uncalled-for, hurtful and tactless."

"I know. In many ways, I wish that I never found it." Without hesitation, this time, Jodi got up, tore the letter into a million pieces and tossed it into the blazing fire. She felt good about doing that.

Jodi returned to the carpet. Mr. Bojangles was not far behind her. Sitting back down, she continued with her questions.

"Do you know Dodo at all?" Jodi asked her mother's friend.

"I met Dodo once at a gallery. She and your dad were in Seattle for its opening. I was there on a photo shoot. She didn't impress me. I couldn't figure out what he saw in her. I remember that she didn't have much style, no pizzazz."

"It all still hurts, all of it." Jodi said ready to renew the crying.

Breaking the spell of the lingering gloom in the room, Jayne nodded her head towards the half empty bottle of chardonnay, *"Come on, we have a bottle of wine to deal with here."* Raising her crystal stemware in the air, she said solemnly, *"Salute, Susie! I love you. Ciao, my dear friend!"* Their canine companion gently raised his head and yowled as if he was joining in their toast.

Jodi missed Jayne when she returned to Seattle. Jayne was a wonderful friend to her mother and now, she was a wonderful friend to her.

Chapter Nineteen:

Oh, My Sister, Passing from Me

JODI PHAN HAD ALL SHE could do to concentrate on her life as it was before she talked to Sgt. Trent. The whole idea that someone would want to kill her mother was preposterous. Her mother did not have an enemy in the world. The only person that she knew of that had ever hurt her mother was her own father. When he left one day, years ago, and ended up shacking up with his former secretary, it tore the family apart. It was a total shock to Jodi's mother. She had no idea that her husband was messing around with someone else. And then poor little Amy had a serious set back.

Amy Johnson was a charming, adorable child. She had large blue, enchanting eyes. Her infectious smile captivated everyone who knew her. All of her teachers and friends were moved by Amy's jest for life. She was beyond doubt, a little angel, cherished by so many.

Amy had brought so much joy to the world. She was also quite the little joker when she wanted to be. She certainly enjoyed clowning around.

One day she was shopping with her babysitter, whose name was Anna Kelley. Somehow, Amy got lost in the mall and she bravely went to the security guard on duty and told them that she had lost her babysitter. The guard asked her what the girl's name was. Soon after, the intercom system blasted, *"Will Anna Banana please report to security."* Anna did not find it humorous. Another time, Amy used all of Jodi's expensive shampoo to give the puppy a bath. That cairn terrier was the sweetest smelling dog in Tompkins County.

When Michael was asleep on the sofa one afternoon, Amy quietly and carefully painted his toenails a very hot pink color. He did not appreciate it at all. He was panic stricken when they couldn't find the nail polish remover.

She also made up a story that her mommy was pregnant. Susan couldn't understand why everyone was congratulating her. When she found out, Susan was mortified! But, probably the most irritating thing that Amy did was to put all of Jodi's bras in the freezer. When Jodi finally located them, she chased her little sister around the living room, flinging the hard as rocks undergarments in the air, as Amy laughed hysterically. The little girl was fun and curious and full of surprises.

One rainy Day, when Amy was about eight years old, Susan asked her to clean her bedroom, which was in quite a disarray. "Now, Amy," her mother warned her, *"I expect you to use a lot of elbow grease."* About twenty minutes later, Amy came rushing into the kitchen, crying wildly. *"Mama,"* she whimpered, *"I have looked everywhere. I just can't find the bottle of elbow grease."* Another time, just as comical, Susan had asked her to put her sneakers in the mud room at her friend's house. After several minutes, she exploded with, *"I don't see any room with mud in it!"* She also told a lady in the neighborhood, who was cranky and grouchy that she really didn't look sour. *"My mama says that you are a sourpuss!"* she proudly told the woman after church on Sunday morning. Susan just about died of embarrassment. It was the idioms that got her every time.

A very precocious child, Amy was always very aware of her surroundings. In first grade, she was sitting at the lunch table, watching her sixty year old teacher slip a few saccharin tablets in her coffee. Always very quizzical, Amy looked at the teacher with her big blue eyes and innocently asked her, *"Don't you want any more babies, just like my mommy?"* She had the saccharin confused with Susan's birth control pills. The whole faculty room was a buzz with that incident for weeks.

That little imp kept everyone laughing and she kept them on their toes. You had not idea what to expect with that child.

Amy was born with a congenital heart problem, called transposition of the great arteries. With this defect, the aorta and pulmonary arteries are reversed. The aorta received the oxygen-poor blood from the right ventricle, but it was carried back to the body without receiving more oxygen. Likewise, the pulmonary artery received the oxygen-rich blood from the left ventricle but carried it back to the lungs.

When Amy was an infant, only a day old, she required a surgical procedure. All patients with transposition of the great arteries have need of surgery in the first few days of life. The infant had to undergo this procedure in the catheterization laboratory to "buy time" and delay major surgery until she could handle it better. The procedure enlarged a naturally occurring connection between the right and left upper chambers (the atria). This let the blood mix so some oxygen-rich and oxygen-poor blood could be pumped to the correct side. Amy survived this procedure.

She underwent a major open- heart repair at thirteen months old. It was frightening. All that Susan could focus on were the gowned figures hurrying in and out of the operating room, their faces hidden by green masks. As she heard one of the cardiologists say as he passed her, "Amy is safely on the heart and lung machine," she felt as if she would explode.

Fortunately, the surgery went well. Amy was able to have a normal childhood. As she grew, she didn't remember her early years and she considered the long scar that criss -crossed her chest to be her "red badge of courage."

She played softball and soccer, took ballet and tap dancing lessons, played the violin joined the girl scouts and spent a lot of time with her friends. She loved to go camping with her mom. They spent every Memorial Day Weekend and Fourth of July in a tent by Fish Creek, near Oneida Lake. Amy relished her time in the woods, building campfires, canoeing, biking, hiking, and roasting marshmallows. Time and again, her mother would swiftly snap a picture of Amy with marshmallow stuck to her face. Amy loved it most when her mother rented a pontoon boat from the campsite and they packed tuna sandwiches, potato chips and bottles of spite in a cooler and drifted along the creek to the mighty Oneida.

At the nearby Sylvan Beach Amusement Park, she loved riding the rollercoaster, lifting her arms in the air and squealing gleefully. She and her mom would end a day at the park by searching for shells on the beach, putting them in zip lock bags so that Amy could pass them out to her friends in school.

Amy loved softball. It was her passion and she also played soccer and she was good at both. She was a dedicated girl scout, selling cookies every fall out of a red wagon that she pulled across the neighborhood, door to door. So pleased of her sash, which was filled with badges and pins, she displayed it proudly across her chest.

She didn't like thunderstorms and she was afraid of lightening. If ever there was a storm, she and her little cairn terrier would cower together under the shelter of her trundle bed. *"Hush, Casey!"* she would warn the pup, *"No barking."*

Sadly, her happy, cheerful life was cut short. When she was twelve years old, rapid growth spurts at the onset of her teen age years put enormous strain on her deteriorating heart. After a week in a hospital in nearby Syracuse, doctors became more and more alarmed as heart medications began to lose their effect. Amy's damaged heart became useless. She went into aggressive heart failure and was desperately in need of a heart transplant.

When her health began to fail and she became too weak to run the bases during her softball games, she told her mother not to worry. *"I will just hit homeruns and walk those bases."* And, she did.

Chapter Twenty:

I Found God Tonight

AMY, WITH HER MOTHER BY her side, was rushed by ambulance to the Columbia Presbyterian Hospital in the Bronx. When they got there, Susan prepared an overstuffed chair in the intensive care unit as a bed for herself. She would only leave her daughter for a few minutes to talk to the man on the steps.

Susan watched in dismay as Amy was instantly attached to an extra corporeal membrane oxygeneration machine to allow her failing heart to function. Mother and daughter were gearing up for a serious battle. The team of pediatric cardiologists at Columbia confirmed that Amy was critically ill.

Being in the hospital changed Susan forever. While there, she experienced some mind altering occurrences. There was a very grubby street person who had settled himself on the stairs of the hospital. He lived in a box, literally. Susan could not figure out why the hospital personnel would allow him to be there. He was a real lost soul. He had a cut-rate bottle of sangria sticking out of a brown bag and he held fast to an old sheet filled to the brim with his worldly possessions. Susan ignored his attempts at making eye contact. She would zip by him as quickly as possible. When Amy realized that her mother was intentionally overlooking the man, she was disappointed. *"Please, don't do that anymore, Mama. What harm would it be to be kind to him?"* Susan informed Amy that you don't go around talking to homeless people in the Bronx. Amy was not convinced. She pleaded with her mother to be nicer to the man. So, the very next time that Susan saw the man, she greeted him openly. He was overjoyed and from that moment on the homeless man from the Bronx and the pained mother from Central New York bonded in a very unusual way.

Ensconced in the intensive care unit, entangled in tubes and wires, Amy's weak and fragile body was tethered to the ECO machine for seven, long, grueling days. Tiny tears fell from little Amy's swollen eyes. Her sounds were unintelligible. Naked, her slender body was covered by a thin sheet. Her eyes were covered with cotton swabs, her lips were badly swollen and a huge feeding tube distorted her mouth. Susan sat by her daughter's bed, grasping her hand, feeling the gentle touch of her long graceful fingers, which slowly wrapped themselves around her hand. Susan was so afraid that if she let go of Amy's hand that beautiful, special bond between them would be gone forever.

Amy was in critical condition, dying. Susan watched helplessly as Amy stopped communication. Her eyes no longer opened in response to her mother. Her tiny hands no longer grasped Susan's in recognition. Amy was gone. Her angel wings were flying with great speed and her immortal heart was pumping strong enough to carry her off into an eternal light.

Susan without delay rushed to the man on the steps. She hugged him very tightly. Through the unpleasant smell of alcohol, body odor and stale cigar smoke, Susan held on for dear life. Some force, unknown to her, drew her to him and through that force, she was able to cope with the agonizing loss that had just befallen her that night.

He was kind and caring. He told her, *"Life hurts. Believe me, I've lived through the worst of it. Because of the war, in Nam, I've seen lots of death and too much suffering. I found out real quick that Nam wasn't about baseball, hot dogs, and apple pie. It was about survival! I've loved and I've lost.*

He paused for a moment and then continued. Susan sensed Mikeys presence. As if he had crossed through a cloud that had separated them and stood there, trying to reach out to her. *"Oh, Mikey"* she thought. *"I need you, now!"*

The man broke the spell and continued. He took her hands in his.

"I didn't always live like this. I used to have a nice home and a great family. I was weak. I gave up. I dropped into a deathtrap, an eternal chasm that swallowed me whole. I stopped living. Don't do that. Don't let this sad, sad tragedy stop you from moving on and from making a difference in this world."

Susan leaned into his shoulder and burst again into a torrential storm of tears. *"Amy asked me several times if she was going to die. I told her that I didn't know. I told her that we were worried. I told her that the doctors would try very hard to help her. She told me not to cry and that she would be waiting for me in heaven. Each and every time, she said that. She knew. She had to know."*

The man took Susan's hands in his. *"The loss of your little Amy is one of the most brutal jolts that you will ever endure. It is an out-of-order process that brings unbearable anguish. You will never, ever "get over" this. You will never be the person that you once were. Amy's death is not a disease from which you can get better. It is a life altering change that you must learn to live with. As a bereaved parent, you have to learn to go forward. Little Amy has found a new home now and that new home is in your heart. She will always be a part of you. You must say "goodnight" to your little angel and pick yourself up and be strong. Amy was telling you that, herself."*

Susan was having what seemed to be an out-of-body experience. The tears stopped. Her mind completely shut down. Amy was gone. Everything that Susan did that night appeared to be happening to someone else. She felt totally numb, both emotionally and physically.

Afterwards, she never saw him again. But, she never forgot him. He was her angel. Her angel sent to her from Amy. All of her life Susan had searched for God in many places. That night she found him in that man's face. She saw friendship. She saw faith. She saw hope. She saw peace. She saw love.

Amy's entire family suffered deeply from the loss of her. Their precious little Amy was gone and it took Susan Johnson several years to be able to face life without her little girl. The pain was too overwhelming.

Some time after Amy's death, when the summer sun came to warm the Earth, Susan journeyed many miles from her home. She traveled, cloistering herself in the solitude and warmth of a quaint, rustic river cottage on the St. Lawrence River. She was drawn to the majestic beauty of the river to contemplate, to meditate and to embrace her memories of Amy.

On her first morning there, the August sun was struggling to warm the slow moving motion of the mighty river. With coffee cup in hand, Susan settled in a large wicker rocking chair on the screened porch of the cottage. The chill of the morning air felt crisp, as she wrapped a disheveled army blanket about her shivering shoulders. Shifting in the chair, she pulled her long legs beneath her, wrapping the blanket more tightly around her. Mesmerized by the beauty of the season, she rocked slowly back and forth. As the river awakened and the dawn brought its sun down from the heavens, Susan fell out of the blanket, like a butterfly emerging from a cocoon. She was in awe of the cloudless sky above her. Gazing upward with outstretched arms, she released her pain. She promised God to serve the world in a way that she could use her talents to benefit other children in need. Remembering the man on the hospital steps, she whispered softly to Amy, *"Goodnight, my angel."*

She thought very carefully about how she could make things different. She wanted to help other people in need. She was a teacher. For the past several years, she had not worked. Being a "stay at home mom" did fulfill her. But, now it was time for her to do something else, something valuable. She found a job with the juvenile detention facility and realized that she was exactly where she needed to be. The man on the steps was right. She could move forward and make a difference.

Why would any one want to hurt a woman like Susan? Who would want to hurt a woman who had been through so much heartache, anguish and sorrow. Most people looked at Susan for strength. They admired her for her courage and felt her pain as she set out to put her life back together.

Chapter Twenty-One:

As Close to True Evil

JESUS HAD EVERY THING FIGURED out. He had made a promise to Manuela and he would keep it. There were four people who were on the list that he gave to Chico. The first name was one that would cause no problem. No one would care, especially the NYPD. One less junkie on the streets was not going to be a priority for them. They would look the other way.

He was Buddy Cruz, a reprobate, a nothing. Buddy Cruz was born Hernando Alberto Cruz, the fourth son in a family of seven boys. He was raised in Miami. When he left home, or was kicked out of the house, no one was sure which happened first, he hitch-hiked to New York to stay with some Puerto Rican relatives in the Bronx.

After a few months, because of his outrageous behavior, he was thrown out of his uncle's house. He called the streets of New York City his home. Sleeping in the doorways of downtown businesses and on the benches of city parks wasn't uncommon for him. Buddy hung out with the worst of the worst: drug addicts, psychos, prostitutes, thieves, and hired guns.

He looked the part that he played. He was filthy. He rarely showered or bathed, cut his hair or shaved. His clothes were grotesque. They consisted of garments worn to shreds that he pilfered from nearby garbage cans.

Buddy had no sense of decency. He had no principles, conscience, ethics or morality. He lived from day to day and would do just about anything for a free meal and a few dollars. As a drug dealer, it didn't bother him at all to string out a twelve year old. He was more animal than man. In and out of jails and mental hospitals, Buddy was never going to improve his lot in life. His dependency on heroin and cocaine ruined his chances for ever getting out of the despicable rut that he was in. He would sell his soul for a dime bag of ice.

Buddy could not remember any other life. When he was a child, living with his parents in Miami, he was a social outcast. He had no friends. Even his brothers would not include him in their games. He was repulsive even then, bad- tempered, belligerent, and confrontational.

When Darren Reed offered him $50.00 and a new pair of Nike joints to drive a truck into a young girl, he greedily accepted the offer and didn't flinch. It was like asking him to bake a cake. He could care less about anyone or anything. He was as close to true evil as any one could ever be.

After he crushed Manuela's body into a nearby fire hydrant, he stopped by the deli for a tuna on rye and then went to collect his money from Darren Reed.

Jesus gave Chico his instructions. *"Hacerlo rápido y limpio. Use un cuchillo y corte la garganta. Asegúrese de que oye el nombre de Manuela antes de morir."*

Cruz had no idea that the girl that he was paid to murder was Jesus Moreno's sister, so he didn't let the connection deter him from meeting with Jesus in a seedy bar on the Boulevard. They had a few beers. Cruz did not notice when Jesus slipped a sedative into his glass. Jesus told Cruz that he had a business deal for him. Cruz was interested.

The two men left the bar, got into Moreno's Benz and drove to a desolate area, where they sat talking for over an hour. The sedative began to kick in and Buddy fell asleep. Jesus left to go pee in the nearby woods. Shortly afterwards, Chico Alvarez came upon the scene, surprising Cruz, he pulled him out of the car and bludgeoned and strangled him to death. Moreno returned, got into his car and drove off, leaving Chico to deal with the dead body. Before, leaving, however, he slipped a roll of twenties into Chico's pant's pocket.

Chapter Twenty-Two:

A Watchful Eye

SGT. TRENT HAD RECEIVED THE records from the phone company that serviced Susan Johnson's cell phone. On the day she died, she received a phone call from 607-347-8854. That number was registered to Barney L. Cole and as luck would have it, he was a guard at the Brentwood Detention Center.

Sgt. Trent traveled to Brentwood in his own car. He didn't want to be seen in an official vehicle to rouse any attention. Grant couldn't accompany him on this trek. The younger officer was busy attending the police academy in Albany, where he was assigned to train the cadets. When Trent arrived at Brentwood, he went through the same procedures to get into the building that he did at Glasswing.

The place was a lot older than Glasswing and it was in really bad shape. It seemed so badly maintained that a wrecking ball could only improve it. The place had been deteriorating for the past fifteen years. State funds were scarce and locally hired carpenters had cob jobbed repairs to the building for a long time. The rooms were dank, reeking of antiseptic smells.

Trent saw more than a few young girls walking together, under the watchful eyes of state guards. The girls were ghost-like, creeping in unison as if in stupors. Trent thought that Brentwood was depressing put side by side with the more modern, sun- filled Glasswing.

Trent's first stop was to see the director, Kay Marshall. Her office was possibly the only bright spot in the building. She had decent furnishings and the newly painted walls were a brilliant blue. Her desk was cluttered, but it seemed like an organized clutter. Kay was a chunky woman with gray hair and unusually common features. Trent was thinking that if he ever saw her again, he would not remember her. There was nothing about her that was impressive. In her early fifties, she wore large black rimmed glasses, a matronly green, polka dot dress and black loafers. Trent was sure that the loafers were comfortable on the concrete that covered the floors. She looked a bit troubled, perhaps over worked and worn-out. She smiled at Trent as he entered her office. She was notified of his arrival by the receptionist and she was bewildered by his visit.

She did not stand, but she removed her eye glasses and set them on her desktop.

"Please, have a seat." she pointed to a couch at the rear of the room." The room was filled with the aroma of freshly brewed coffee.

"Coffee," she offered. Pointing to a Mr. Coffee on a side table. *"I just made it."*

He had already had his coffee for the day. He shook his head, taking a seat in the plush softness of the over stuffed sofa. *"No, thanks."* She got up and poured herself a cup.

After a few sips, she set the coffee cup on her desk and sat down, swiveling the chair around from side to side a few times before Trent began his questioning. She gave him a blank look.

"I will make this a quick visit," Trent said with no emotion. *"Thanks for seeing me at such short notice."*

She grinned, still perplexed. *"How can I help you, Sergeant Trent?"* She clasped her hands beneath her chin as if to steady her head.

"Do you have an employee here, named Barney Cole?"

"Yes, we do. He works the ten to seven AM shift in one of our South Wing cottages. May I ask why you are asking?"

"I will get to that," Trent snapped in a crisp tone. *"First tell me if cell phones are allowed in the program areas by your staff."*

"No," she answered sharply, still unsure of the questioning. *"We prohibit any mobile phones any where in the buildings or the cottages. They are considered contraband."*

With further questioning, Trent determined that Cole was indeed working the evening that Susan Johnson died. Kay Marshall checked the time sheets that were neatly arranged in a file cabinet in her office.

"Yes, Barney was here that night."

"Now," Trent thought, *"things were getting very complicated."*

Trent thanked Kay Marshall for her time and left the facility. She immediately made arrangements to meet with Cole the very next morning.

After some preliminary questioning, Cole owned up to having a cell phone in the building.

Trent was a lion with the heart of a kitten. After visiting the two juvenile detention centers, he wondered, *"What the hell went on inside them."* Curious, he decided to find out. He had some connections in Albany and he managed, without too much difficulty, to get his hands on the state evaluations for both facilities. He was satisfied to see that they were rated very highly.

The educational, medical and psychological services, counseling, mentoring and training opportunities were all top notch. The ability to provide follow-up post placement services was excellent and the recidivism rates were improving. The dining center provided delicious foods with vegan and vegetarian options and there were accommodations made for children with food allergies.

The staff was dedicated and rarely used punitive measures in dealing with the youth. Trent was fully aware that children break the law. He was also aware that they needed reliable adults to serve as their mentors and to offer them opportunities to make affirmative adjustments to set things right. He was glad to see this was all happening at Glasswing and at Brentwood. But, then when he remembered Susan Johnson, he knew that she would never be a part of an organization that did not put the children first.

Chapter Twenty-Three:

Here Comes that Rainy Day Feeling

BARNEY COLE WAS STARTLED WHEN Kay Marshall called him into her office right after his graveyard shift at Brentwood. It was a hectic night and he was dog-tired and starved. He gulped down a jelly donut and had a couple slurps of coffee before he got to her office. "Marshall must have gotten in at least two hours before her expected arrival time this morning," Barney guessed. As a rule, she pulled in her reserved spot at about nine o'clock. He punched off the clock at exactly 7:02. This meeting must be important because the director never asks to see the staff unless they are getting promoted or fired. A promotion would be nice. He and his wife, Jenny had three kids now, a fat mortgage and two hefty car payments. Their credit cards were maxing out and a little more money in his pocket every month would help. He heard that there was an opening in the stockroom and they were looking for a new foreman in the purchasing department. Both of these positions were a pay grade higher than his guard job. Now, he was smiling.

But, Kay Marshall was not smiling when Barney got to her office. In fact, she was visibly upset. The questions crashed into him like a bombardment of gun fire from a machine gun. He was noticeably nervous. Marshall did not invite him to sit.

"Yes, he did have a cell phone in the building."

He didn't know where this was going and how much information Marshall had. He knew he better fess up to the cell phone.

"My wife was pregnant and due any minute. What would you do? I needed the phone and then someone took it from my backpack. I couldn't even report it missing because I wasn't supposed to have it."

"Yes, it was missing for awhile."

"Yes, it had been returned to his backpack."

"No, he had no idea who took it."

"No, there were no out of the ordinary notations for calls "dialed"."

She made him feel like one of the kids. He expected her to throw him into cuffs and shackles at any moment.

Yes, he would think real hard and try to remember anything that might help. But, it was a year ago.

Now he had to go home to tell Jenny that he was on three months probation, without pay. Damn!!

Kay Marshall had to eat some crow and call Sgt. Trent to tell him that one of her employees did not follow policy.

Chapter Twenty-Four:

Sometimes it Feels Like it's Raining all Over the World

ON THE TWENTY MINUTE DRIVE home, Barney thought about how awkward it was going to be to tell Jenny about his probation. That was really going to throw them behind in their bills, which meant excessive late fees and past due charges. She was going to be so worried about it all. He also thought about how hard she had worked as a receptionist in a dental office before the kids started coming. Having three babies in five years took its toll on her and now this set back was going to really disappoint her.

As he came in close proximity to their modest home on a small cul de sac in Ithaca, he looked it over carefully. It had four good sized bedrooms. There was a large one car attached garage, a full walkout basement, a shed and a workshop. They had an enclosed year- round front porch and an enclosed three- season back porch. The setting and views were very extraordinary. They could see a smidgen of Cayuga Lake from the front porch. Barney parked his car in the garage and walked directly from the mudroom to the large, spacious kitchen. Jenny loved this kitchen with its custom oak cabinetry, tiled floors and pretty red and white gingham curtains on the large window that faced the fenced in garden.

She was stationed by the sink, still dressed in her blue, flannel housecoat. Her long brown hair was coupled in a loop at the top of her head. She was pouring coffee into a large mug. Emma, the one year old was sitting in her high chair, making a mess with a bowl of cheerios, flinging them helter skelter about the room. The older two, Erin and Max, were eating their cornflakes and drinking their orange juice at the round, maple table. The first one to see him enter the room was Max, who put his chubby, three year old hands together and gleefully broadcast to the others, *"Daddy is home."* Erin ran to him and embraced him. He picked her up and gave her a big, bear squeeze. Then he kissed Max on the top of the head and pecked the baby on her cheek.

"Hi hon," Jenny said glancing in his direction. *"You are late this morning. Problem with one of the girls?"*

He rested there for a split second, his six foot, two hundred pound frame, leaning against the refrigerator. Barney was rock-hard muscle, no excess weight. He looked like a giant next to his petite wife, who only just tipped the scales at one hundred and ten pounds. They had met in high school and he marveled at how she managed to keep her small frame regardless of her three pregnancies.

Once Jenny settled the kids down and sent them to the den to play, Barney sat next to her at the kitchen table and told her about the cell phone, the meeting with Karen Marshall and the probation.

She was noticeably distressed. She put her hands to her face and moved up and down gently in her chair.

No words could convey how sorry he was.

Barney used up the remainder of the day trying to remember. The only thing that stood out in his mind was that Manuela Moreno had Susan Johnson's phone number. One day, he was mandated to work a double shift. He was on duty when Susan Johnson was there. He could picture Susan writing the number down on a piece of scrap paper for Manuela. It meant zero to him at the time.

Manuela had by now left Brentwood. In fact, she had been in some sort of accident, injured pretty gravely, maybe even killed. He heard some talk about it. But, since he worked the graveyard shift, he wasn't privy to all of the hearsay at Brentwood. However, he would forward the information on to Karen Marshall.

Marshall, in turn, gave the information to Trent. Trent, straight away, wrote a letter to the NYPD, inquiring about a possible connection between Moreno and Johnson.

Chapter Twenty-Five:

Falling into a Burning Ring of Fire

CHICO HAD NO DIFFICULTY FINDING Darren Reed. All he had to do was ask a few questions. The homeboys that he spoke to confirmed that Reed was a real wangsta. In street talk that meant, "fake ass gangster." But, Chico didn't really expect him to be as scruffy and disheveled as he was. He knew a lot of pimps from the barrio and they were usually very polished, all studded out in bling bling and name brands. Reed, on the other hand, looked more like a person in exile from a third world country.

Chico spotted Reed sitting in an espresso bar on Lexington, talking to a young girl, about fifteen years old. She was weeping and he was acting supportive, cheering her on. Chico heard Reed mention, *"safe haven and sanctuary and shelter,"* as he held the girl's hands in his."

Chico eavesdropped some more. Darren held the girl by the arm as he led her out of the building.

"Sugar, yo boyfriend is wack. Cha know what I mean? Yo is da bomb, yo is kickin' ass! Yo hang with me and the Benjamins will fly, girl. Now, let me tell ya what's goin' down tonight, baby."

Chico scoffed at Reed, *"Este tipo es una bolsa de suciedad. Ese chico no tiene la oportunidad de llenar su hell. He es con tal basura."*

This job was not only going to be a painless one, but one that would help everyone in el barrio.

Darren Reed was walking out of the *Backstreet Cantina*, a neighborhood tavern, when he turned off the beaten path to take a shortcut through a remote, out of the way road behind a barbershop. It was dark with nightfall's eerie shadows walking up and down the sides of the buildings. No street lights penetrated through the narrow passageway. Chico couldn't have asked for a better place to take action.

Darren did not see what struck him. Two blows to the back of the neck with a switch blade and Chico was convinced that it was over. He doubted that there would be an obituary and he doubted that there would be much of an investigation.

After the vigorous attack, Chico called Jesus on his cell phone,

"El trabajo está hecho. Usted puede estar tranquilo a mi amigo. Voy a estar ahí para mi poco dinero y la próxima misión."

The next day he collected what Jesus owed him.

He slept very well that night.

Chapter Twenty-Six:

When Silence is the Only Sound

JESUS HAD FOUR THINGS TO do on Sunday morning. First, he went to call on his mother. She was always thrilled to see him. They had a brief visit. She smacked him on the butt on the way out of the house, like she had done ever since he was a child. And she said the same thing that she always said when he left, "Jesus ser bueno. Haga su mamá y papá orgulloso."

He came back with, *"Sí, mamá, siempre estoy bien. No se preocupe,"* kissed her tenderly on the cheek and left.

His second stop was the graveyard, where he was deep in thought, pensive, mulling things over. Silence was the only sound there was.

The third thing on his 'to do list' was to check the weather forecast in Ithaca, NY. Snow storm predicted for the 7th. *"Good,"* he thought to himself.

Last of all, he made arrangements to get a message to Sassy McQueen. She was still at Brentwood. She was released about six months ago and locked up again. after not passing a court ordered drug test, breaching the provisions of her early release. After the test, Sassy was holed up in a shoddy Harlem hotel until the cops trapped her sleeping off a drinks and drugs binge. They also found an elbow of weed in her possession.

Jesus hit on a girl from Queens who was being shipped to Brentwood the next day. He gave her a letter, advised her to sew it into the lining of a Bible. She would be strip searched when she got there. Nobody would question the Bible. If they did check it out, they wouldn't find the letter. Her instructions were to hand the Bible over to Sassy McQueen. This cost him. The girl wanted $500.00. It was worth it.

Chapter Twenty-Seven:

Sassy's Song

WHEN THE GIRL FROM QUEENS arrived at Brentwood the following day, after all of her intake procedures, she looked for Sassy. Luckily, she was assigned to Sassy's cottage. As soon as she had the opportunity, she gave Sassy the Bible. Jesus had warned Sassy that she would be getting a letter. "You will find it where only God has been."

Sassy read the letter carefully. It took her a moment or two to figure out the words. Jesus was careful to write it as if he was writing to a first grader. He knew Sassy's limitations.

She didn't read well or write legibly, but she was very good at committing numbers to memory. It was a valuable skill to have on the street. She saw the numbers that Susan Johnson wrote on the scrap paper she gave to Manuela Moreno. Sassy took a brief look at the numbers, recording them everlastingly in her mind. The numbers were 607 746 8815. Sassy repeated those numbers over and over in her head at least a hundred times.

"Sassy,

Get to a phone on the 7ᵗʰ. Call the number. Do what we talked about. J."

Sassy knew what to do. She also knew that Cole would be on duty that night. He might be a problem. He was always watching everybody like a hawk. But, Hinkle would be his partner. Hinkle was an easy target. Sassy would wait until Cole went to take a leak. She would ask Hinkle if she could please get some toilet paper from the supply room. He'd let her. Cole's backpack would be hanging on the back of the door. She saw it there before. She also knew that he had been carrying his cell phone in that bag ever since his wife got knocked up. She and Jesus were counting on the cell phone being there. This was going to be simple. She would disguise her voice. She could do that OK. She would call the number and tell Susan Johnson that her favorite kid, Carlos, over at Glasswing was melting down. Sassy would be believable. She would then delete the call on the cell phone. The rest would be up to Jesus.

Chapter Twenty-Eight:

The Weight of Lies

CHICO HAD A LOT TO do before the 7th. He made plans to rent a car, using a stolen ID and credit card and reserve a hotel room in Ithaca. He settled on the Park Side Motel about twenty minutes from Susan's house. It was a seedy "pay-by-the-hour" dive. He registered there under the name, Bill Maxim, the poor clown that he stole the ID and Visa card from and he told people that he was an insurance salesman. He needed a few days to stake things out.

He kept an eye on her house, watched her every move. He figured that it would be easy to get into the garage. It had a side door that she never locked. Since he didn't need to get into the house, the locked doors at the front and side of the house would not be a matter for concern.

Chico was worried about the foot prints that his heavy Timberline boots would make in the snow. But, the blizzard was coming into the area so rapidly, the tracks would be concealed under a layer of fresh snowfall.

For three nights, he watched to see when the lights went out. Susan was predictable. The lights went out at the same time every night, 11:30 .

All he really had to do was be quiet. He could cut brake lines in his sleep and loosening the lug nuts was easier than dealing with the brakes. He did it. It was done. No big deal at all. Now, all he had to do was keep an eye on the house from the street. Sassy would call. Soon the lights would go back on and the garage door would open. The car would drive down the slick, treacherous roads.

Chico would have felt some shame about this job. But, since he never met the victim, he didn't feel remorse at all.

The next two jobs would be a bit delicate, especially Jimmy Dentes. It is never easy to have someone stiffed in lock up. But, Chico and Jesus would find a way.

Actually, Chico was thankful that he didn't have to pull the trigger on the kid himself. He remembered Jimmy from the neighborhood. He was a good one; smart, polite, even-tempered. He didn't belong in the hood. He definitely didn't belong in the pen. He was probably being eaten alive in there.

Jesus had a contact in lock up who could do the job. All Jesus had to do was visit the guy in prison and talk to him for a few minutes, sealing a deal. Lenny Turango could make the arrangements on the inside. Lenny owed Jesus a few favors.

Chapter Twenty-Nine:

Dancing With the Devil

SASSY MADE THE CALL. SHE was pleased with how she had convincingly changed her voice.

Miss Johnson was on her way. That is what she said, *"I will be right there."*

Having Jesus in her corner would make things a lot easier when she bailed out of the hell hole she was in. He had some influential friends in the Neta's organization. She needed friends on the outside, especially cop friends. She needed a crooked cop to change the results of her drug tests.

She heard about how smart Jesus Moreno was. Well, she really pulled the wool over his eyes with this one. She knew how protective he was of his sister. All Sassy had to do was tell him all about how Miss Johnson was harassing and stalking Manuela, berating her, criticizing her, and most recently, putting the make on her. Manuela would never testify about what was happening. Who would believe her over the sainted, well- respected and admired teacher?

" I sho ain't fibbin' yuh, Jesus. Things ain't real tight here for yuh sistuh. Yuh know real well, that all this crap comin' down here with Miss Johnson, ain't doin' Manuela no good at all. That bitch is really buggin!" Sassy screeched in her hip hop slang.

Yes siree, Jesus sure didn't like hearing all that. It was all lies, of course. Malicious and spiteful lies, made up by the sick and scheming criminal mind of Sassy McQueen. She was swollen with pride. After all, payback is a bitch.

Chapter Thirty:

Putting Two and Two Together

JIMMY DENTES REMEMBERS HOW HE appreciated living in el barrio when he was a kid. He enjoyed the diversity and multiplicity of cultures and the vivacious and invigorating way of life. He loved the bumpin' hip hop music that came from the street corners. He loved the smells of ethnic foods that flooded the area. He loved everything about his childhood. As he grew older, his outlook changed. He began to see only the sorrow that spread through the streets. He saw the corruption, the hardship, and the grime and devastation that put all of the populace in jeopardy. He learned to hate living in a neighborhood where he had to dodge bullets.

Jimmy was smart. He was well-educated and he knew that there were better things out there. His mother often reminded him, *"Jimmy, if you are educated, all your dreams can become real."* He heeded her words and dreamed of getting out of the ghetto and moving upward. He dreamed of moving to New England, where he could live by the sea and watch the fishermen dock their boats and haul their catch to adjacent markets. He dreamed of lush summers to walk on the beaches. He imagined brilliant autumns blanketed with gold-and-red colors and crystal-sharp winters. In the spring time, he would plan hikes in the countryside or peaceful walks through the village greens. He longed for the quiet, the serenity and the historical experiences that he could have there. He wanted to get married after college and have children, who were able to go to the best schools and have the finest things. He was willing to work hard to accomplish his dreams. He soaked up everything that he could from reading and studying and listening intently to his teachers. His future was promising. He was different from the others in el barrio, not because he wanted out, but because he was going to do it the right way.

Everything changed for him on that fateful day when a cell phone call and a text message shattered his dreams. He should have been paying better attention. He knew that. He would give his right arm to have Julia Valdez back. He would regret that day for the rest of his life.

Prison life was difficult for him. It seemed that no one trusted him. He was a loner. He spent most of his leisure time reading, working on his GED and writing letters to his mother and to his appeal lawyer. He was guarded and suspicious of everyone and checked off the days he had left on a wall calendar. They were all the same, the days; mind-numbing and friendless and fear-provoking.

Jimmy's constant fear of violence had a major impact on the quality of his life. He was seldom free from the fear of intimidation or bullying. Even most of the guards were unpleasant. One day, he asked a passing guard for the time. The man snapped back in a crushing tone, "What the hell do you care. You ain't going no where." That was the kind of handling of prisoners that was typical. And what he got from the other inmates was far worse.

He had heard from his sister that his former girl friend was in college. She had pursued her dreams. He had deterred his, maybe forever. She was at Buffalo University. She was happy and she and her new boy friend lived in an apartment together in a Buffalo suburb. At first, she wrote to him and then gradually, over time, the letters stopped. He couldn't blame her for following her dreams and getting on with her life. He was happy for her.

The only person that Jimmy talked to at the prison was the chaplain that came from a local Catholic church once a week. The two men had high- spirited, intellectual and thought provoking conversations. Jimmy looked forward to the chaplain and that was about all that he had to look forward to.

A surly, brusque, and burned out officer on duty at the mess hall was the first to hear the scuffle. There were yelling and banging sounds and shrill, uneven breathing coming from the kitchen. Jimmy Dentes and Lenny Turango had been in the kitchen dishing out mashed potatoes from a giant pot on the stove. When the guard arrived in the kitchen, Lenny was bleeding from the nose and Jimmy was laying face down with the handle of a knife sticking out of his shoulder. Jimmy was breathing. The 911 call was made.

Soon afterwards, an ambulance and several EMTs arrived at the prison. Lenny was immediately cuffed and put in isolation until Jimmy could tell his side of the story. Lenny, of course, called out, *"self- defense."* But, no one believed that the placid, composed and easy mannered Jimmy could be at fault.

Chico and Jesus were infuriated when they heard that Lenny had botched the job. Things could get really out of hand if the Feds pressured Lenny too much. He might weaken and spill everything. That could mean that Chico and Jesus might be incriminated in the deaths of Susan Johnson, Darren Reed and Buddy Cruz. Someone just might put two and two together.

Chapter Thirty-One:

Out of the Gutter

A HOMELESS WOMAN WHO WAS thrashing through a trash can behind a bar on the boulevard screamed hysterically when she unavoidably brushed against the body of Buddy Cruz, which was buried underneath the mountain of rubbish. He had been gagged with packing tape. Furthermore, a urine sample revealed an unusually high level of gammahydroxybutyrate - a drug, which can be used as a sedative.

His body was identified, tagged and stuck in a morgue on 115th Street. Ironically, Buddy sent a message to the police. The coroner found a piece of paper stuck in Cruz's sock. It contained a message, still intact, despite Cruz's body being dumped in the trash and covered with debris. The paper had been folded several times over. When it was unfolded, it became apparent that it was a reminder to meet some one at 10:00 PM on February 12, 2000, the day before Cruz disappeared. The note simply said: *Meet J.M. at 10:00 on 02/12.*

The New York police were starting to get interested in the recent homicides in their precinct. It looked like someone was trying to rid the world of the city's most unsavory. They were going to put their top detective on what they called, the Dirt Bag Murders. He was Jason Greene, a long time, veteran cop. If there was any kind of link or the possibility of a serial killer, Jason would sniff it out. He was a blood hound when it came to "who done its." And, he got right to it.

Greene was a fifty two year old detective, who was not at all prepared for retirement. He loved what he did and did it well. His colleagues expected him to die at the desk. The seasoned cop was committed to his job. Single, with no attachments, his work was his life.

He was a large man who didn't seem to fit in a suit. His paunchy belly fell over his belt, the hems of his pants, tattered and soiled, touched the floor. His ties were constantly mangled in disarray and his shirts, though laundered and pressed, looked crumpled and shabby on his full-size frame. His hair was thick and snow white. Too long, it hung over his ears and fell at the nape of his neck, falling chaotically on to his shirt collar. His eyes were a deep sapphire and they looked as if they could see straight into your soul. He was slow motion, walking as if he was on a treadmill that was going at a snail's pace. Greene was never in a hurry. He took everything in and his surveillance and scrutiny skills were razor-sharp.

Greene sat down in his sparsely furnished office, thoroughly examining the mound of files on his disorganized desk. It would take him several hours to clear the detritus in front of him. Reading the files over and over, he struggled to ascertain how the victims could be connected.

Reed was a pimp. Cruz was not. Reed was Puerto Rican. Cruz was Dominican. They both lived in el barrio, approximately four miles from each other. Cruz's crib was in a housing project. Reed lived in a run down, pay by the night, motel. Not much to go on. There was no fundamental difference between the two men. They were both dirty. There had to be a connection, he could feel it.

For days, Greene tried persistently to pull the case together. People have said that the world's greatest inventions have been discovered by accident and this proved true with great detective work, as well. As Greene was clearing the clutter from his desk, he came across a file from the Tompkins County, NY sheriff's department. He had been so engrossed with the Dirt Bag Case that he neglected some of the other material on his desk, marked, "URGENT."

The Central New York detectives wanted Greene to see if there was any connection between Manuela Moreno, killed by a hit and run driver a year ago in Spanish Harlem and the suspected murder of a Susan Johnson in Ithaca. They supposedly knew one another. Was there any possible way that Moreno could have been involved in any illicit transactions with Johnson? They thought that it was a long shot, but they would be pleased with any support that Greene could provide.

It didn't take Greene long to figure it out. Manuela was Johnson's student at Brentwood. She was the sister of Jesus Moreno, a Neta big wig and power head for the Spanish Harlem community. Manuela was a hooker with Darren Reed's harem. It was reported around the ghetto that she squealed on Reed when she was in lock up. Reed was being tailed by the NYPD because of the information that she fed the cops. His pimping business was under the radar and he was losing thousands of dollars. Buddy Cruz was a junkie and the gossip from Greene's informants was that Cruz was the hit and run driver, who killed Manuela. Now, the puzzle was starting to fit together.

Chapter Thirty-Two:

All I Could Do Was Cry

JIMMY WAS IN A LOT of pain. He had a surgical procedure to repair his injuries. Lenny's brawny physical power had crushed into the flesh of his shoulder, breaking bones and tearing tendons. He felt awful, still groggy from the pain medications. He was shocked by what had happened. He had no idea why Lenny would assault him. What was his gripe? He didn't have a clue. He didn't even talk to the man. The two of them were just doing their job in the mess hall, dishing the slop of mashers onto plastic plates. Lenny never said a word to him and vice versa. In fact, Jimmy ignored all of the inmates at Walton. He just wanted to put in his time, go home and try to put his life together again. He was not interested in making friends.

Jimmy saw the cops in the corridor of the surgical wing of the hospital and his heart sank. He was not in the frame of mind to be interrogated. He was sore all over. His whole body withered with pain. The meds they were giving him, didn't seem to be doing their job in alleviating the painfulness of his wounded shoulder. When the police entered his room, they got as comfortable as they could in the two rigid, straight back chairs that were hiding behind a bed curtain, that separated Jimmy from the other patients. Sitting formidably by the curtain was a state armed security guard, standing out like a sore thumb, making sure that Jimmy didn't try to escape. Jimmy found it quite amusing that the state was paying this guy an hourly wage to sit and watch over someone who couldn't move.

The police were vigorous in their questioning. Jimmy told them exactly what happened. The state guard perked up, listening with curiosity. The arrival of the cops eased his boredom a bit. He hated this hospital gig.

Jimmy, shifting his bruised body, trying to get comfortable, began telling his side of the story. He had turned his back on Lenny for a second, as he reached for more plates. Out of the blue, he felt a razor-sharp throbbing slice through his shoulder. Instantly, Jimmy turned back around, startled. He glued his eyes directly into Lenny's face, as the other man was about to reach for a butcher's knife that had been placed in the steel wash basin. *"How the hell did that knife get there?"* Jimmy remembers thinking. Immediately, he put his strong athletic body to good use, laying a violent blow to Lenny's face, making the man cup his hands beneath his bloodied nose. Lenny's eyes narrowed as he felt Jimmy's knee come hard into his groin. Overwhelmed, he squashed the wounded, dazed Jimmy down to the ground. Somewhere voices began to scream and cry out at them. That was all Jimmy could remember. He assumed that help arrived, the ambulance was summoned and he ended up in a hospital bed, feeling wretched.

Jimmy also told them that he didn't want any problems with anyone. He just wanted to mind his own business, follow the regulations and get out of corrections. The police checked Jimmy's records and he was clean. He was a model inmate. Like he told them, he didn't want any problems with anyone.

Of course, Lenny's depiction of the incident was entirely unlike Jimmy's. He pointed the finger at Jimmy for making the first move, taking the first swing.

Since there were no witnesses to the attack, the outcome was inconclusive. Jimmy was moved to another unit of the prison and Lenny was taken out of isolation.

There was no way that Lenny was going to be able to get to Jimmy.

Chapter Thirty-Three:

Pretty Woman

GREENE WENT TO VISIT JESUS Moreno. Moreno owned a small pawn shop on the Boulevard, which Greene suspected was a cover for a Neta gambling enterprise. Jesus had to be in the horse and sports betting business. He had a lot of high-priced things and he rolled with classy broads. Gaming was the way to haul in the big bucks. One rainy Monday morning, Greene sauntered into the shop, which was located inconspicuously between a greasy short order diner and a sleazy adult video store, two blocks from the Boulevard.

Sitting behind the counter, was a stunning red head. The beauty had fair features, large indigo eyes and a pleasant smile. Her clothes were exquisitely tailored and tastefully fitting to her slender, long-limbed frame. Crimson locks draped down her back in a carefully pulled together ponytail. She wore a silk, red dress and had several gold chains that dangled loosely about her throat. Large golden hoop earrings hung gently from the lobes of her ears.

Greene noticed that her finger nails were freshly manicured and she looked more like an ivy league law student than a pawn store clerk in a crack neighborhood in Harlem. Greene asked her if Mr. Moreno was available and she said that Jesus was out of town for a few days. She asked if she could help him. Did he have something to pawn? Greene told her, *"No, thanks, everything is good."* She smiled and Greene left, thinking that he wanted to yank her out of there and position her right in the middle of Fifth Avenue so some well-known model agent could see her and change her life forever.

Remembering Jesus, Greene was disappointed, he wanted to put the fear of God into him. He chuckled to himself by that. Was it an oxy moron to want to *"put the fear of God into Jesus?"* Greene guessed that Jesus's mother had high hopes when she gave her son that name.

Detective Greene came to the conclusion that Jesus Moreno was significantly implicated in the murders of Darren Reed, Buddy Cruz and Susan Johnson. He concluded that it was a Mafia- type "eye for eye" vendetta. But, how could he prove it?

He delved further into Manuela Moreno's bio and everything seemed to come together. All of the murders were, in some way, connected to her.

He was at a standstill. His gut told him one thing and his criminal investigating mind told him another. He had the solution and wasn't able to prove a damn thing. It irritated the hell out of him.

Chapter Thirty-Four:

A Wee Bit of Good Luck

THEN, SOMETHING TOOK PLACE THAT changed his luck.
Greene got a call from Rev. Tim O'Brien, the pastor of St. Martha's
Church at 1858 Hunt Ave. in the Bronx.. Greene and O'Brien had
been friends since college. The two graduated from Notre Dame
University in the late 60's. Greene went to work as a foot cop in
Manhattan and then bumped his way up to detective. O'Brien
became a local assistant pastor in Queens and later became the
high priest of St. Martha's. The two men kept in touch through
the years and Greene would, now and then, talk about his cases
with the good father. O'Brien's brilliant mind, coupled with his
good judgment, made him the perfect person to bounce ideas off.
This time, thrashing over the case with O'Brien, proved to be very
worthwhile.

As soon as Greene told O'Brien about the Dirt Bag Murders,
adding Susan Johnson into the mix, O'Brien became fascinated
and made a decision to do some of his own snooping around.

He, not knowing that it would be pertinent to the case, returned a phone call to arrange a meeting with another clergyman, who needed some information. The other man turned out to be, none other than, Bill Vickers, the chaplain for Walton Prison. Vickers was a stout, jovial, man with no hair on top of his head. Predominantly, above his mouth sat an outrageous grey handlebar mustache. He wore his clerical dress regally, and was void of any adornment, except for a long string of rosary beads, which fell all the way downward to his bulging belly. O'Brien thought that Vickers looked exactly like a barbershop quartet's lead singer, disguised in a clerics robe.

The chaplain wanted to meet with O'Brien to discuss one of the men from St. Martha's who had recently been sent to Walton. Vickers said that the prisoner, Antonio Pronti, was worried about his family. He wanted some information about his wife and children. Pronti was concerned about how his wife was going to pay the rent and keep up with the other bills. After meeting the woman, Vickers offered to consult O'Brien who was their family priest. He was hoping that O'Brien would be willing to arrange for some support through the local assistance programs.

Pronti's wife vehemently claimed that her husband was a good man and a wonderful father. She said that he faithfully abided by the seven sacraments of the church. When hard times hit the economy, he lost his janitorial job at one of the schools. Falling into a financial downspin, desperate men do desperate things. He started working for some local thugs. He was their look- out when they hit up a grocery store. Regrettably, the end result was disastrous.

A sale's girl in the store was shot and critically wounded. Antonio got three years of hard time.

The clergymen met at Luigi's Italian Restaurant in Harlem. The food there was excellent. They ordered drinks before dinner. Tim O'Brien selected a bottle of Coor's light and the chaplain opted for a glass of Canadian Club and water. The men hashed over the specifics for awhile before dinner.

"Do you know the family? Vickers wanted to know.

"No, I don't know the Pronti family. But, we have a large congregation," O'Brien answered.

Do they attend mass regularly?" O'Brien was interested in the answer. People tended to look to the church only in times of misfortune.

"She says that they do," Vickers answered. *"She and the four kids, for sure."*

"Do the children attend catechism classes? Have they all been baptized? Does the father provide for religious training at home? O'Brien was spitting out a succession of questions.

Vickers was happy to respond with, *"Yes, yes, yes to all three questions."*

"Good, good, good," O'Brien chortled, *"Glad for that. The church will do all we can for them. Don't worry. I will pay my respects to Mrs. Pronti tomorrow. Where do they live?"*

Vickers took a pen from the pocket, hidden beneath masses of black fabric that made up his clerical robe. He reached across the table for a napkin and jotted down the address. O'Brien slipped the napkin into his coat pocket.

O'Brien was happy to give some assistance to Pronti's wife. Catholic charities could help with the rent and he could find a way to help with the other bills until Pronti got out of lock up. His parish had a large sum of money in the bank just for such predicaments. O'Brien advised Vickers that Pronti must be on his best behavior at Walton. If the man could get an early release, the church would try to help him find a job. In fact, they could use an experienced janitor to help the housekeeper in the rectory at St. Matha's. It wouldn't pay much, but it could get the man back on his feet.

When the waitress arrived, they had already perused the menus and decided on their orders. The chaplain chose manicotti stuffed with cheese and baked with homemade tomato sauce and mozzarella with a side salad of cucumbers and tomatoes drenched in a balsamic vinegar. O'Brien was eager to try the seafood pescatore, which was linguine and red clam sauce gently sauteed in a bounty of scallops, shrimp and fresh mussels with a Caesar salad, laced with anchovies. After their entrees, O'Brien ordered a decaf and a shot of sambucca and the chaplain ordered regular coffee and Tuscan Tiramisu, a umascarpone cream layered with ladyfingers soaked in kahlua and coffee syrup.

While having their after dinner treats, the conversation turned to other topics. The two men discussed an upcoming Yankees game, their views on the recent economic situation, their common interest in Ted Kennedy's health reform campaign and some church related issues. Vickers began talking about a young man at Walton, who was sentenced for vehicular manslaughter.

"He is a great kid, no priors and his conduct in prison has been terrific." Vickers relayed to O'Brien. *"Recently, he was assaulted*

and injured. He's convalescing in the hospital and is expected to have a long recuperation period."

"Wow," O'Brien was eager to hear more. *"So, how did a kid like that end up at Walton?"*

"He was involved in the death of a Spanish Harlem girl a year ago. It was an unfortunate accident. The kid was set up with a hanging judge and ended up in corrections." The chaplain wondered if O'Brien knew Julia Valdez or possibly, Manuela Moreno. They lived close to his parish.

"Manuela Moreno", that name was so familiar to O'Brien.

"Oh, my heavenly God! That was the name that Greene had mentioned in the Dirt Bag Case."

"How was Manuela connected to the boy at Walton,? O'Brien wanted to know.

With a somber gaze, O'Brien soaked up every bit of information that Vickers fed him.

Jimmy Dentes.

Lenny Turango.

Jesus Moreno

Everything was starting to make sense. What a huge twist of fate. Greene was going to be interested in all of this.

O'Brien stood up, unexpectedly.

"Please, excuse me," he whispered to the chaplain. *"I have to make an important phone call right now. Enjoy your dessert. I will be right back."* Smiling, he knew that he was on to something big.

Greene was in bed, drowsy from watching the eleven o'clock news, when his phone rang. The only light in his room came from the television set. Groping for his reading glasses, his eyes focused on the red numbers that danced across his clock radio. Eleven- forty six. He fumbled about the end table to find the phone, answering it on the second ring.

"Greene, here." he uttered in a monotone. O'Brien spoke quickly and precisely. *" Sorry that it is so late. I have some very interesting news for you, Jason. You are going to love this. I think that I have another apparent attempted murder that can be connected to Jesus Moreno."* O'Brien told Greene all about Jimmy Dentes, the driver of the car, which killed Manuela Moreno's best friend. He told him all about Lenny Turango and his assault on Jimmy Dentes. He told him that Turango had one visitor while at Walton and that visitor was Jesus Moreno.

"What a coincidence," Greene thought to himself. *"Or, maybe, not a coincidence at all."*

Greene was certain that with this new bit of information, he could put the squeeze on Lenny Turango to cough up the truth.

Chapter Thirty-Five:

Gripping My Heartstrings

JODI PHAN STILL SLEPT RESTLESSLY, tortured by dreams that she could not remember. She needed some answers. Being out of the loop way too long, she decided to contact Sgt. Trent. She wanted to know how the investigation into her mother's death was going. She and her family deserved some answers. Neither Jodi nor Mike had heard from Trent in weeks. Trent was in his office when she called. He took her call, without delay.

Glancing at the heap of clutter on his desk, he shuffled the papers to locate some notes that he had taken on the case. He told her that things were at a stand still for some time. He had only just a few days ago held a telephone conference with some people on the staff of the NYPD. They were in the process of investigating the connection between Jodi's mother and some gang members in Harlem. It was still not clear to him what was going on. He would contact her when he knew more.

Jodi was stunned. It was ridiculous! Her mother was a nonviolent woman. Susan, often with one or more grandchildren in tow, spent her free time following trails into the backcountry to enjoy sleeping under the stars. She would pack a canoe and paddle out to an island to sleep at the water's edge, taking in glorious sunsets. She loved the sounds of nature from inside a rustic cottage. Her mother was known to travel to the splendor of New York's beautiful Adirondacks or to the shores of Oneida Lake at Sylvan Beach. She enjoyed the breathtaking joy of a riverboat cruise on the picturesque St. Lawrence and touring Montreal by a bus, returning on her own to stay at the Auberge Pierre Calvert for several days after the tour. Susan loved the beauty of nature, steeping up every breathtaking vista.

When she wasn't working or traveling or playing with her grandchildren, Susan used up the rest of her free time visiting her mother, Jodi's grandmother, in a local nursing home. Susan would sit in a chair at the Cherry Point Nursing Home for hours, just gazing at the older woman, wishing that she could pull her back into the world. Jo Deligrossi was diagnosed with Alzheimer's disease. All the elderly woman could do was sit in a chair by a window, letting the sunlight warm her tormented body. Her fingers would fidget fretfully as she opened and shut them, over and over again. As her lips quivered, she fell into a mysterious darkness all of her own. No one entered her world. She was lost there, by herself. Susan would sit and watch as her mother spit and drooled and picked at her chapped lips. Susan felt a deep loneliness every time she visited her mother. She realized full well that her own mother had no idea that she was there. Her own mother had no idea who she was.

Placid memories of Nonna rushed back into Jodi's mind like a soothing burst of fresh air on a blistering summer day. It was so hard-hitting as Jodi watched her grandmother become more and more out of touch with reality. Confined to a nursing home, the once outgoing, enthusiastic woman now had limited intellectual ability, which caused her to communicate with cries, mumbles and moans. She was no longer able to respond to any one and she required total support for all functions of daily living.. It was so awfully difficult for the family. Jodi cried after each visit with her Nonna. She missed Susan, who had always been there for her with consoling, comforting words.

Jodi had memories of her Nonna and of her mother safely slipped away in the inner most chambers of her heart. Remembering the stories that they used to tell her, one story at a time, made her feel so much closer to them and to all of the women in her family that came before her. Every tale came storming back to her so that she could cherish and embrace it. Probably the most compelling and gripping story of all was the one about her great-grandmother on her father's side, who had died at childbirth.

The poor woman, who was nine months pregnant, had suffered for days with constant pain in her lower abdomen. There was no doctor in the small village where they lived. She had no one to consult, except for a few local women. Those women from the neighborhood, who were assisting her were self appointed midwives. They were convinced that she was in labor.

Eventually, her appendix ruptured and peritonitis set in, causing tachycardia, rapid and shallow breathing, and severe restlessness. Unable to help the baby along, the midwives grew increasingly alarmed. They finally sent someone after a doctor in a nearby town. Unfortunately, it was too late. The woman, Jodi's great-grandmother, died. She was buried in the same coffin with her stillborn son.

The lonely great-grandfather soon afterwards, traveled to Italy to find a wife and mother for his other three sons. The Italian woman that he married was a widow with a small daughter of her own. The newly married couple and the little girl journeyed on a ship from Rome to America.

The trip was arduous. They were in steerage. Rats were everywhere and a fowl, nauseating odor flooded throughout the ship. By the time they reached the welcoming sight of the beautiful woman holding the torch, they were exhausted, sick and filthy. After lugging their possessions onto barges that would take them to Ellis Island, the two adults with the frail little girl by their side, were tagged with information from the ship's registry and passed through long lines for medical and legal inspections to determine if they were fit for entry into the United States . As others passed through without problems, they were detained for days. They watched, nervously, as others traveled by barge to railroad stations on their way to destinations across the country.

Finally, they were updated as to what the hold up was all about. Due to some legal entanglements, the little girl was unable to enter the country. Because Jodi's great grandfather had not adopted the child in Italy, the American officials were forced to send her back to her home country. This was a horrible situation.

The great- grandfather's new wife could not go back with her child because she was married to an American citizen and her young child could not stay because she had not been officially adopted. It was just an oversight on someone's part that turned into a devastating conundrum. Immigration police had to wrench the wailing child away from her mother, who was overcome with grief. The little girl was frightened and alone, feeling abandoned. On the return voyage, the child became terribly sick. She was vomiting profusely and was dehydrated and pathetically frail. Without any one to look after her, she almost died. When all of the officially authorized paperwork was finally completed, she refused to embark again on the long and grueling journey. She opted, instead to remain in Italy with relatives of her deceased father. She never saw her mother again. This riveting tale always gripped Jodi's heartstrings.

When she thought back, Jodi remembered her own mother as a woman who led a peaceful, quiet life. Susan didn't hang out with criminals or mobsters. She hated the city and urban life frightened her. She enjoyed losing herself in the wilderness.

The only contact that Susan had with gang members was at her job at Glasswing. The realization of it hit Jodi like a ton of bricks!

"Oh, my God," Jodi was in a state of shock. *"The whole thing had to do with Glasswing. How in the world could this happen?"*

Lenny's testimony was going to be the only evidence that the prosecution had. He was not a model witness by any stretch of the imagination. Jesus could dig deep into his pockets to get the best lawyers in the city. His legal representatives would have Harvard degrees, decorating their Fifth Avenue offices. They would condemn Lenny, stating that he extented a "cloud of impropriety" in the court room. They would argue fiercely that there was no evidential grounds to arrest Jesus Moreno, except for the affidavits of an unreliable criminal.

Lenny presented himself astutely in front of the judge. He donned a new suit and tie, compliments of the State of New York. He got a haircut and was clean shaven. He intended to choose his words carefully. But, the beads of sweat still formed on his forehead when he entered the stately courtroom.

The prosecutor was a headstrong, gifted young lawyer, named Mike Gianelli. He was a straight arrow, graduating from Cornell Law School at the top of his class. It wasn't Harvard, but it was damn close. He was a whiz kid, hot headed enough to establish a hell of a case. He was determined to send Jesus to prison for a long, long time. Giannelli was thirty years old, but looked ten years younger. Poised, confident and charismatic, he bristled when people compared his natural good looks to that of the handsome actor, comedian Charlie Sheen. *"I think I probably act more like him than look like him,"* the outspoken Giannelli would chuckle, expressing amusement at the comparison. Giannelli threw himself into the trial. He devoted every minute to it.

His biggest undertaking was to make sure that the members of the jury didn't have their judgments clouded by Lenny's criminal record. It was going to be a long shot. If he was a high stakes gambler and put money on himself and won, he'd be a very rich man. The odds were probably fifty to one. But, he had the gambling spirit and he was going to give it everything he had.

Lenny had accepted a bribe from the prosecution. He was going to get three years off his maximum sentence and state protection for two years after that. He fessed up and told Trent and Greene every thing that he knew about the Dirt Bag Murders. He was probably more terrified of Chico than he was of Jesus. But, Chico wasn't on trial, not yet. This one was all about Jesus.

The trial was given front page coverage in the city papers. Reporters and cameramen planted themselves in front of the courthouse. There was chaos and commotion while curiosity seekers lined the narrow street. The Dirt Bag Murders that some how involved a peaceful teacher from upstate was causing pandemonium in New York City.

Chapter Thirty-Six:

In Walked an Angel

JESUS SAT IN THE COURTROOM, cuddled up between his ivy league attorneys, wearing a Bottega Veneta navy blue suit, a white pinstriped Giorgio Armani shirt and a red silk necktie designed by Satya Paul Design Studio. His highly buffed shoes were Georgetowns by Allen Edmonds. Flaunting his extravagance, he fixed his eyes on his Rolex from time to time, giving the facade of being uninterested. Giannelli thought that what Jesus deserved was a fresh -out- of - college public defendant. But, he had the money to hire the big guns.

As the trial progressed, Gianelli became more and more troubled. It bothered him to have Jesus in the courtroom every day. He would sit, flanked by his expensive counsel, smug and pompous. Jesus knew that most of the top cards were in his deck. He held the aces. Giannelli's deck was full of jokers. But, Giannelli did have some marked cards to play with. He had some valuable affidavits to present to the jury. Several people had prearranged depositions for both the defense and the prosecution. Their written statements were read in court.

FOR THE PROSECUTION:

Lyle C. Spencer, automobile mechanic;

"Yes. I inspected Susan Johnson's car. The lug nuts and the brakes had been tampered with."

Matthew Patrick Hastings, neighbor of Susan Johnson;

"I did indeed see what appeared to be a silhouette near Susan Johnson's garage on the night that she died."

Barney Cole; Security Guard, Brentwood Residential Center;

"I did see Susan Johnson give her phone number to Manuela Moreno. Sassy McQueen was in the room at the time."

William Alexander Maxim;

"My driver's license and Visa card were stolen and I reported them missing after they were used at the Hertz Rental Agency and at the Park Side Motel in Ithaca, NY. on or about the time that the victim was in the fatal accident."

During a painstaking search of Chico's residence by the police, a pen, a book of matches, and a napkin were recovered. They were all from the Park Side Motel in Ithaca, NY. A telephone number for the Hertz Rental Agency was written on a slip of paper and attached to Chico's refrigerator door with a magnet. William Maxim's Visa card and driver's license were also there, hidden beneath the mattress of Chico's bed.

Greene couldn't believe that Chico would keep any of that stuff. *"What a self-assured son of a bitch he was."* It was also very interesting and quite weird that the cops found a manila envelope underneath that mattress. The envelope contained an oval shaped sterling silver St. Christopher medal with a broken chain, a wallet with a few bills in it and a Class C driver's license, issued to a Tomas Moreno.

Walter K, Emmert; Bank Manager First Security Trust Company;

"Chico Alvarez did make three large cash deposits in our bank around the time of the murders."

The police uncovered the bank statements from his residence.

Detective Greene snickered to himself, *"That wasn't too smart of you, Chico. I would have figured you for more of a pro than that. Nobody in the hood puts their money in a bank. Shame on you!"*

Sam Powers, Visitation Attendant at Walton Correctional Facility;

"Lenny Turango had only one visitor at Walton and that visitor was Jesus Moreno."

Now Greene is visibly in high spirits, *"Smart move bringing this guy's affidavit before the jury. This really ties the knot around Jesus's neck."*

Alexander Keller, Coroner, New York City;

"I did indeed find a note in the sock belonging to Buddy Cruz while undressing his bludgeoned body. The note indicated that Cruz was meeting some one with the initials J.M. the day before he disappeared."

Greene is snickering. *"J.M.",* he thought. *"What a coincidence!"*

FOR THE DEFENSE:

Angelina Marie Ortega, girlfriend of Jesus Moreno;

"On the evening that Susan Johnson died, Jesus Moreno was with me from 7:00 PM to the following morning."

"Hell, who are they kidding," thought Greene. *"That doesn't prove a damn thing. We are talking about a hired gun here."*

Joseph M. Patterson, Manager of the Park Side Motel, Ithaca, NY;

"On the day in question, no one by the name of Chico Alvarez registered at our hotel."

Greene is grinning from ear to ear, *"Holy shit, the defense is grasping for straws. Giannelli will bury this one. Of course Chico would use an alias. The shit that they found in his apartment pretty much puts him at the dump, anyway."*

Jesus did not testify at his trial. Defense attorneys will almost always call as a witness an articulate client that they believe to be innocent. Since they didn't call Jesus to the stand, it looked good for the prosecution. That was the one good thing that Giannelli had going for him. He needed a lot more than the circumstantial evidence that he had. He had to start peeling the layers off the onion.

The only sentiment and sympathies that the jury would sense would be in regards to the untimely death of Susan Johnson. It was still uncertain why she was one of the victims of Jesus's rampage. Lenny only knew that she was one of Chico's hits. He had no idea why.

It also bothered Giannelli to see Jodi Phan and her brother, Mike, sitting there day after day, bewildered and overcome with sorrow. They still couldn't phathom how their mother could have ever been messed up in all of this chaos and drama.

Only a miracle was going to turn the tide of events. After a week of disappointing sessions in court, Giannelli got his miracle.

The chitchat in the corridors of the courtroom was that Giannelli had a surprise witness that was going to pull the plug on Moreno. Gianelli had worked day and night. He finally found an ulcer in Moreno's body that was about to rupture.

Everyone in the courtroom was still when she walked in. She sat directly next to Giannelli. A bit apprehensive about being in the room with Moreno, she took a few fleeting looks in his direction.

"With your permission I would like to call the witness, Emily Evers to the stand," Giannelli declared, looking directly at the judge.

"Permission granted," the judge responded.

Every eye was on the stunning young woman as she walked slowly towards the bench. She was dressed in a navy blue suit, with a wisp of white showing at the neckline. Her skirt was ankle length and she wore navy Prada sling back shoes. She had a single red brooch in the shape of a heart fastened to the lapel of her bolero type jacket. The brooch was embedded with cultured pearls. Her hair was her crowning glory. It was a rich scarlet, long and silky and smooth. As she approached the judge, she tossed her head slightly to flick an unruly piece of hair away from her eyes. The eyes were like an azure pool, floating on her pale, flawless face. Her lips were full and luscious, glossed lightly with a hint of red. Her hands were long and slender and they were extended in length by glossy, red fingernails. She wore a dazzling marquise cut solitaire engagement ring on her left hand. Why was she there? Why was she willing to testify?

Chapter Thirty-Seven:

Take These Chains from my Heart

SITTING IN THE VERY BACK of the courtroom was Jason Greene. He had been there every day, waiting for the top to blow off the case.

"Good God," thought Greene as he recognized the girl from the pawn shop. *"There is going to be one hell of an explosion."*

Greene quickly looked at Moreno as Emily reached the stand, standing their gracefully, right hand on her heart, *"I swear to tell the truth, the whole truth, so help me God."*

Moreno looked upset. One of his attorneys was whispering in his ear. Moreno started to rise, the fury showing as the red blood in his veins colored his face. His attorney put his arm on Moreno's shoulder, guiding him gently back into his chair.

Emily was ready to tell her story, but it was not without some trepidation. Was she nervous? Yes. Was she going to show it? No.

As she began to testify, Greene's ears perked up, he leaned forward, and everything else in the room faded away.

Emily Evers was born in a small town in North Eastern Pennsylvania on the New York State border. It was a railroad settlement that united three small towns to form what people called, "The Valley." Simply put, it was a great place to grow up. It had great schools, award winning health care, beautiful homes, and a variety of jobs and shopping alternatives. The lush farmlands and the historic downtown areas made it a wonderful place to live.

Emily lived with her parents in a large 1890's Queen Anne Victorian home in the center of Athens, PA, one of the triple cities of the valley. The home was regal and fancy — famous for its flashy embellishments. The house had a steep roof, shingled insets and slanted bay windows. Flourishes to the home included lots of gingerbread, spindles, ornate cornices, brackets, and stained glass windows. Emily felt like a princess in her pink bedroom with its white wicker furniture and teddy bear collection.

Emily's father was a specialist with an esteemed team of oncologists at the highly regarded Robert Packer Hospital. Her mother was a stay at home mom, who kept her self busy with volunteer work, her darling daughter and an occasional round of golf at the country club. Emily's parents prepared her to always do the right thing. They advised her to look into her heart whenever dealing with a complicated predicament, to come to a decision based on what would best help her sleep at night with no misgivings. Emily lived by her parents' advice. She was a responsible, straightforward, and honest young lady.

Shortly after Emily graduated from Athens High School, she packed her suitcases and scampered off to New York City with her boyfriend, Ryan Hamill. They were a striking couple. He, with his blonde hair and cerulean eyes, large muscled frame and rugged features and she with her gorgeous red hair, sapphire eyes, fair skin and supple, sumptuous body. They were young and in love. He was off to New York University to study business administration and she was enrolled in a world renown modeling school on Fifth Avenue. They were happy.

Soon after they arrived in the city, Emily began to look for a part- time job to earn extra money. Their parents had been paying most of the bills. However, the two students, wanted a little extra to use for vacations and other leisure activities.

Emily interviewed with Jesus Moreno for a job in his pawn shop. It seemed like an easy way to make a few dollars. All she had to do was wait on the customers. Ryan did not like the neighborhood and he was a bit suspicious of Moreno.

"That guy looks like a thug to me." he cautioned Emily.

But, it was better money than any one else was offering, so she took the job. Still doubtful, Ryan would drive Emily to and from the sordid hood every day.

Emily was not aware of anything that went on in the back area of the building. People entered there with special key cards from an outside entrance. Sometimes, she would hear boisterous commotion and see a multitude of people, going in and out. She minded her own business, collected her pay check every week and forgot about the place when she wasn't there.

Moreno who loved fashionable, chic things around him, was happy to have the beautiful, young woman dress up his dreary, lackluster shop with her pretty smile and sophisticated appearance.

Moreno was respectful to Emily. He knew she had a boyfriend and he never put the make on her or acted with any impropriety at all.

The arrangement worked out well for everyone. Until the ill-fated day that Emily will never forget. A man, named Chico Alvarez turned up in the shop. He and Jesus went to talk behind closed doors in a storage area behind the counter. Unaware that a vent was left open, their exchange was able to be heard throughout the shop. Initially, Emily made an effort to pay no attention to the men. However, things rapidly got out of hand. She became panicky and frightened as she heard about the gruesome murders. She concentrated on the names and committed them to memory; Sassy McQueen, Lenny Turango, Darren Reed, Buddy Cruz, Jimmy Dentes, and Susan Johnson. She remembered the dates, times and status of each contract killing. It was horrifying, bloodcurdling.

She escaped the shop early that evening, feigning a headache and immediately went to Ryan with the information. He was terrified for her and tried to ease her anxieties. He cautioned her to be quiet until they could talk to a lawyer. The very next day, they met someone on Madison Avenue. He listened cautiously and advised them to wait a week or two, until Emily had time to quit her job. They did not want Moreno to be suspicious of her.

She packed the few things that she had in the shop; a tote bag, some mouthwash, a bottle of liquid sanitizing soap and a pair of reading glasses. She gave a week's notice, telling Moreno that the job was interfering with her classes. He believed it.

She never saw him again until the day that she made her grand entrance into the courtroom. She was promised around the clock security and the Neta network was on twenty four hour surveillance. She was doing the right thing. When Moreno and Alvarez were convicted, the Netas would forget about her. They really didn't have any stake in the murders. They were simply involved, through association, to a revenge killing spree, orchestrated by Moreno.

Greene was smiling again, *"We got the bastard!"*

Chapter Thirty-Eight:

On the Highway to Hell

JODI PHAN LISTENED INTENTLY TO all of the questions, motions, probings, and inquisitions. She still had no idea how her mother became one of the victims. Emily did not have an answer for that either. Perhaps, they would never know. Perhaps, she was just in the wrong place at the wrong time.

But, that was not good enough for Jodi. She was yearning to get to the bottom of it. Every time she heard the term, "Dirt Bag Case," she cringed. The expression was so unfitting, so distasteful.

The only persons who could give her the reason were Moreno or Alvarez. And, who was Sassy McQueen? Everybody was asking that question. Finding the answer to that question was something that Greene would embark on himself.

He unearthed her in a squalid slum on the corner of Vine and Hudson Streets. She was out cold, sleeping off a drunken spree and cocaine binge. Greene had to cover his nose with a hanky as he entered the foul-smelling flat, filled with a disgusting stench.

He recognized cat urine, intermingled with body odor, puke and stale cigarettes. It was stomach-turning.

He waited there, watching her filthy body, lifeless and limp. He took note of the continuous rattle of her breathing, with snorts and groans coming from her foul wide opened mouth.

He waited patiently for several hours. She finally began to stir, opening her slits of eyes, coughing a tobacco induced phlegm into a smutty pillowcase. Gagging relentlessly, she puked a yellow, slimy liquid into an ashtray by the soiled mattress that she slept on. Twisting her repulsive body into a fetal shaped ball, she gasped as she saw him there.

It didn't take Greene long to unravel the sequence of events that led to Susan's demise. Sassy was forthcoming with the info when Greene guaranteed her full immunity for her participation in the co-conspiracy with Jesus Moreno. He also slipped two twenty dollar bills into her clammy hands, to secure the deal. Sassy twisted her mouth into a toothless smirk.

Susan's family was grateful to Emily Evers for the courage and strength that she presented in the courtroom. But, it was no comfort to them to make real that the loss of their mother was due to the scheming and deceptive hand of a mindless, embittered, mentally crazed street addict. The whole thing was pointless, tragic. The anguish that Jodi and Mike experienced was insurmountable. Nothing would ever be the same.

Chapter Thirty-Nine:

Bravo!

THE TRIAL DRAGGED ON FOR several weeks. Jodi was near exhaustion and on several occasions, her brother had to help her up from her chair to steady her feet. It had taken its toll on both of them.

Halfway through the first day of the trial. Jodi serenely meandered to the cafeteria and filled a paper cup with hot coffee and sugar. She gulped a few advil and picked up a granola bar. That bar was all she had eaten that day. Michael tried to encourage her to go to dinner with him at a nearby restaurant. But, she couldn't. She hoped that she had the audacity to see this through before collapsing.

Sitting on the bench was Her Honor, Judge Sonia Herkimer. Herkimer, a true arbiter of justice, was a brilliant African American woman in her early sixties. She graduated from Cornell University in 1974 and before her judgeship, she was a professor of law at Georgetown University Law Center. She wore her gray hair in loose curls that covered her head in a chaotic mass. Her granny type glasses plunged to the tip of her broad nose. Her black robe concealed a plump build. Her jovial personality and sense of humor made her popular with most of the attorneys who argued in her court. She was sharp witted, but she did not tolerate any nonsense. She addressed the jury and scanned their profiles carefully before beginning the trial.

When Sassy McQueen was dragged into court, everyone's mouth opened and everyone's jaw dropped. She spilled all of beans, burying Jesus in them.

The twelve men and women were uneasy, sitting restlessly directly to the left of the judge's bench. Swaying to and fro, they were like a bunch of grapes clinging to a vine. The large number of motions and objections and cross- examinations made them weary and weak. These individuals, who were indiscriminately forged together from all walks of life, focused as best they could on the attorneys who argued back and forth. They were there as proud citizens, fulfilling their civic duty to determine the fate of Jesus Moreno. Among them were, a laid off dock worker, a hairstylist, a kindergarten teacher, a grocery store clerk, a waitress, a retired postal worker, a college student, a valet attendant, a bartender, a fashion editor, a draftsman and a grocery store manager. Misty eyed, Jodi Phan spotted one or more of them glancing at her from time to time. Were they looking straight through to her broken soul? She hoped that they saw the pain that she wore like a heavy overcoat. Mike Johnson was all tied up in a knot, afraid that if he let go of Jodi's trembling hand, she would burst into a million pieces.

In her purse, Jodi kept in safe keeping a letter that connected her with her mother. From time to time during the trial, she would glide her hand into her purse to softly stroke the letter, as if it gave her strength to carry on. She had just received it the week before. It was from a little, eight year old girl from a dairy farm in the Rochester area. Her name was Krystin Gates. It was a thoughtful letter, written in the unsteady hand of a small child, adorned with cute drawings of kittens and sunflowers. The sentiment was moving and encouraging. Susan had been an organ donor. After the concerns with Amy, she was a steadfast proponent for organ donation. Following Susan's death, her lungs, heart, liver, eyes and kidneys were immediately put on ice and shipped to various hospitals in the state. Little Krystin was the recipient of the heart and the lungs. Ironically, her congenital heart deficiency was very similar to Amy's. Jodi found solace in knowing that her mother took part in helping to save that sweet child's life.

Dear Jodi Phan,

Thank you for my new heart and lungs.

I am doing a lot better now. I am out of the hospital. Your mother was so nice to give me her organs. I will always thank her for it. My mommy and daddy and sister and my dog will thank her too. Now I can run and play and have fun riding my bike. I can grow up and be a super star ice skater at the Olympics. I love your mother and I love you. I am sorry your mother died.

Krystin Gates

Victor, New York

PS Write back to me. PPS Dace says HI. Dace is my dog

Benny Deligrossi sat in the courtroom one row behind his niece and nephew. He took copious notes and never once looked in the direction of Jesus Moreno. It was a form of showing his disdain for the man. As if it would tarnish his soul, he could not look at the face of the man who destroyed his sister.

He had lost both of his siblings in tragic deaths.

His brother had lay in a bed in a hot and smelly army base in Viet Nam, having no family there to say his, *"goodbyes"* to. His body was shattered and broken by an explosion. He died alone, scared and in pain. And then, his sister was wrenched from him so suddenly. He missed them. Benny also longed to have his mother back. Her illness had taken her away from him. She didn't even know that Susan didn't visit her any more.

In complete control of her courtroom, her honorable Judge Herkimer, took a quick look at her watch and tapped her fountain pen nervously on her desk. Remembering Giannelli's reputation to be long winded, she reminded the prosecution to keep their closing statements to a minimum. Giving Giannelli a thoughtful look, she pointed the pen in his direction and whispered, *"You do not have all day, Mr. Giannelli. Select your words carefully."*

The jurors were glued to the edge of their seats when Mike Giannelli wrapped up his final plea to them. He painted a heartfelt portrait of the committed teacher who tried so hard to turn her students' shattered lives into pieces that fit together again. He lamented about the personal tragedies that she had suffered. He described how Susan had cradled her dying child, tethered to wires and tubes, as doctors fought tirelessly to revive the little girl's failing heart. Giannelli also expressed grief over how Susan lost her brother, a soldier, to the trenches of a war torn country in the rice fields of South East Asia. He went on about how she was the caretaker for her mother, who was worn to shreds by the ravages of dementia. He likened Susan to a saint as he moaned about her many efforts to save wayward young boys. *"Susan,"* he said *"was a woman of peace."* He emphasized her struggles to find tranquility in life once more. She was looking forward to the future when Jesus Moreno crushed her out like a cigarette on an asphalt road. He ended with, *"Jesus Moreno is lower than a tic on a dog."* During those closing arguments, several of the members of the jury wiped away tears. At one point the jury foreman put his head between his hands, simply staring down at the floor. Judge Herkimer raised her eyebrows several times. *"This young attorney used a lot of sensationalism. He was good, damn good,"* she thought to herself.

Emily Evers was a reliable witness. She was squeaky clean. She had absolutely no reason to benefit at all from testifying against the defense. Sassy and Lenny's testimonies would be less reliable because of their own criminal records.

After just an hour and a half, the foreman of the jury faced the people of the courtroom. He glanced at a prepared statement,

"On behalf of the State of New York, we the jury, find the defendant, Jesus Raphael Moreno guilty as charged of three counts of murder and one count of aggravated assault."

"Bravo," Greene was elated.

Judge Herkimer sentenced Jesus to the mandatory fifteen years to life in prison, added a four-year enhancement for the assault and battery inflicted on Jimmy Dentes and imposed more than $526,000 in restitution fees.

Jesus, who would not be eligible for parole until he turned eight-eight years old, showed no emotion before being led away to prison. He was going to be a very high-profile inmate and there was a question of how others would treat him in custody. Everybody managed to get a few enemies in the slammer. Jesus's attorneys asked that their client quickly be transferred from the county jail to a state prison.

Chapter Forty:

Memories Exploding from my Mind

THE ROOM REMAINED SILENT, EXCEPT for the shrill, penetrating cries of Juanita Moreno, Jesus's mother. She sat alone to the rear of the courtroom. The woman's sorrow was carved into the crevices of her face as if the fine point of a sculptor's tool had put them there. Years of poverty, abuse and pain concealed all of the prettiness that was once in that face. Her unruly shock of auburn hair stuck out from under the edges of a knitted skull cap. Dark sunglasses veiled large brown eyes, red from crying. Her petite stature was hidden under the large over sized navy pea coat that swung lightly as she glided discreetly out of the courtroom all alone.

She lingered briefly in the lobby of the court house and after a few minutes, she elbowed her way into the crowded street. She stopped for a moment, pulled a pack of Virginia Slims and a lighter out of her coat pocket, lit a cigarette and after taking only a few drags, dropped it to the ground and snuffed it out with the heel of her brown loafers. Stuffing her hands into her coat pockets, she eased herself into the steady stream of pedestrians that raced across the busy intersections.

Flashbulbs exploded all around him as reporters pushed themselves towards Giannelli as he left the courtroom. They begged him for a comment. He was ready to make a statement.

"This is just one trial. We've got another one to go, but today, our thoughts and prayers are with Susan Johnson and her family. Alvarez's trial has not yet been set. Remember, he, too, is charged with capital murder. We are not done with this, yet." Giannelli calmly continued, *"It's been an emotional trial, .and because of the victim, you know, the victim was an innocent woman. And that was hard to set aside and simply stick to the facts. When the defense got hold of things, the proceedings moved along pretty quickly. The defense's total case was argued in about 45 minutes and 50 minutes was spent on closing arguments. The jury got the case at 4:05 pm and were done about an hour and a half later. That means the jury spent more time deliberating than the defense spent arguing its case. Moreno never took the stand. They simply had no defense. There's no defense for what he did. The only defense that could have existed would be a psychiatric defense, but they had no psychiatric testimony."* He thanked the press and looked about the area, hoping to see Susan's family.

Continuing on her way, Juanita Moreno ambled along increasing her stride to a brisker pace and in her mind, she went back to a place where she used to be. Her thinking traveled to a teeming apartment building where people were horded together like a swarm of bees. She raced through the memories, lots of them. There were cracked walls and cockroaches swimming in the night, neon lights blinking on and off from a nearby pub, and stray cats slinking the length of an alley.

There was Tomas, her former husband, cruel and insensitive. Why had she continued to love him? Why had she felt such grief the day they fished his battered body from the depths of the river? Slaughtered like a pig, she could not even look at the ravaged corpse in the county morgue as the black bag was unzipped before her eyes. Jesus could though. *"Yep, that's him,"* was all he had to say to the coroner, showing no emotion at all as he fixed his eyes ephemerally on the grotesque cadaver.

She had tried on so many occasions to persuade Jesus to get psychological help. But, he refused. There was nothing she could do, except to pray for the best.

Juanita half smiled as she brought back Jesus and Manuela, just toddlers. The good times came back to her. Her babies romped behind her as she fastened sheets to a rope that stretched from an anchor of the porch to a pole beneath a walkway that went no where. The children would tug on the hem of her skirt, whimsical and fun loving.

The memories exploded from her mind like fireworks on the Fourth of July. Birthday parties with chocolate cake and strawberry ice cream, Christmas mornings with stockings stuffed with teeny surprises, Easter Sundays with plastic eggs filled with candy kisses, Valentines filled with little sweet hearts, and giggling children, cooling off on hot summer days by running through water sprinklers. Why was it that all Jesus could remember were the bad times?

As a final point, she arrived at her home, a neat and cheerful bungalow, a sanctuary that Jesus acquired for her to rid her of her misery soon after Manuela was killed. It was located on a quiet lane, smothered in sweet smelling lilac bushes and strategically located lamplights. Old elms lined the streets and red geraniums filled window boxes underneath shiny black shutters that outlined the windows.

Jesus had wanted her to *"enter a new tomorrow."* She entered that new tomorrow with a dead daughter and a son in prison. She longed for her *"better yesterday."* She was sorry for what her son had become. She hated that he was so beaten with bitterness that all the sweetness that was once there was sucked out like the juices of a tangerine. Alone and empty, she felt nothing.

As for Jesus, the red in his eyes and the rage in his heart would carry on. In the end, it would finally destroy him. Prison life would cut off his life lines, tearing him into shreds. He would have to live with the demons that would inhabit his soul.

For their cooperation with the police, Sassy and Turango were given full immunity in the Dirt Bag Case. Sassy crawled back into her grungy hole, living like a rat in a sewer, existing on the refuge of others.

Lenny continued out his sentence at Walton, feeling abandoned and lost. Every day, he wrote a letter to his little girl. Everyday he waited for a reply. Everyday, he was disappointed.

Chico was a survivor. He would be okay, even in a top security prison. He would be able to run his racket from the inside. He knew, from the beginning, that this whole mess with Jesus was going to go down real hard.

One day, out of the blue, at the Westbrook Penitentiary, Chico was shocked that he had a visitor. It was Matilda Alverez. She came to him in peace with the news that his father had passed away. His sadness at the news was apparent to her as he sat back in his chair. He rubbed his forehead, shook his head back and forth several times and sighed deeply. They had a brief visit that was strained, but cordial. As she was leaving, she remembered something that she wanted to tell him,

"By the way, Chico there has been some news of your mother. It seems that she is living in The Pinehurst Reconstruction Home in the Bronx. She suffered a massive stroke. Poor thing is no better than a vegetable! She found a bludgeoned body in a garbage bin somewhere in an alley. The shock of it shattered her. Poor thing! I guess the city is taking care of her now."

Chico could not believe that, in the end, he had actually caused the demise of his own mother. He wasn't sure if that made him happy or sad. Matilda had no clue that Chico was the one who had stuffed the body of Buddy Cruz into that garbage hole. Or, did she?

Trent, Greene and Grant stood in front of the courthouse like triumphant football players, huddled together after the big game. They were pleased with the outcome. Starting with just a set of brakes and lug nuts, they were able to unravel the grizzly chain of carnage, a bloodbath coordinated by Jesus Moreno.

The chaplain told Jimmy Dentes about the killing spree. Jimmy was shocked and distressed that an instant of error on his part had caused a chain reaction of heartbreak. He would be out of prison soon. He would some how make amends for everything.

Emily Evers and her new husband traveled far from the seedy pawn shop in East Harlem. Moving to Washington State, they lived beneath the splendor of an array of diamonds dotting the sky. They enjoyed glorious mountain views and the hypnotic hum of the mighty Pacific to allure them to sleep at night. Ryan accepted a lucrative position with an insurance firm in Seattle and Emily was happy to get some free lance modeling work with a well established photographer. And, she had no regrets.

Mike Giannelli had won the case when Emily Evers entered the courtroom. He could have softened the plea, but he didn't because of them. Jodi and Mike and Benny were there and he owed them a big bang of a closing argument.

As soon as the judge's gavel hit the hardness of her desk, dismissing the jurors, Jodi Phan and Mike Johnson left the confines of the court. On their way out, they ran into Giannelli. They were glad to be able to thank him for everything. Jodi was whip lashed with questions as the press headed in their direction. Feeling a need to protect Jodi, Giannelli cut them off. Dismissing them with his hand, his voice was firm, *" Ms. Phan has no statements for any one today."* Jodi was grateful for Giannelli's intervention.

Benny Deligrossi followed them onto the street. After hugging Jodi tightly and shaking Mike's hand, he embraced Giannelli, thanking the young attorney for the kind words about Susan.

"My sister would have been a bit overwhelmed with all of the compliments that went her way in there. She was quite humble. Quite extraordinary. Thank you. You are one hell of a public prosecutor."

Giannelli was very honored to have the veteran Benny Deligrossi, a prominent trial lawyer commend him that way. Giannelli advised Mike and Jodi not to attend the trial for Alvarez. Giannelli was quite surprised that the judge didn't sentence Alvarez in abstentia. But, she opted for the trial, which shouldn't take long to hear.

"Go home. Hug your kids and get on with your lives," he told them. Mike looked at Jodi. He was going to let her make the decision about that. After a few minutes considering it, she said quietly, *"My brother needs to get back to Nevada to his family. He has three little girls who need their daddy. Uncle Benny is exhausted and so am I. I miss my husband and my kids. We will trust you to hang Alvarez."*

"Don't worry," Giannelli assured her, *"You have my solemn word on that one. We got the revenge seeker and next it will be Alvarez who is going to prison. Greene did some digging, which connects Chico to something else. I can't talk about it, yet. But, Chico can look forward to a long stay in lock up."* After giving hugs all around, Giannelli walked to a local bar with some of his assistants to celebrate. Giannelli had a Lagavulin and branch water on his mind. He needed some relaxation and the scotch single malt should do the trick.

Once on the street, Benny flagged a cab for the airport. He was relieved that the trial was finally over. As he entered the cab, he merely said to the cab driver, *"JFK airport. US Airways terminal."*

Hot off the press, the city papers boasted the headlines,

"REVENGE SEEKER SENTENCED IN DIRT BAG MURDERS!"

Chapter Forty-One:

Can I Taste the Milky Way?

TAKING DEEP BREATHS, JODI AND Mike walked to a nearby parking lot to retrieve Mike's car. He opened the passenger's door for his sister and she got in. They drove the five hour drive back home without talking. They both needed to be alone with their thoughts. Stopping only once, they bought some flowers at a floral shop and topped off the gas tank of Michael's trailblazer. Susan got out of the car to fetch the flowers, while Mike put the gasoline nozzle into his gas tank and pumped forty dollars worth of gas.

Once back in Ithaca, they drove directly to the cemetery, which was located on a hill in the nearby town of Cortland. They felt relief to be there. They were home.

As they drove through the cemetery gates, they saw hundreds of headstones that were next to hundreds of burial places. Row after row. Deligrossi after Deligrossi. So many of their family members were buried there; great- grandparents, grandfather, aunts, cousins, Uncle Mikey, Amy and Mama.

They eventually stopped at the top of the hill near a large elm tree, that shaded two familiar graves. Susan's two children, clutching one another tightly, gently placed two yellow roses encircled with babies breath, at the foot of each monument. Mounds of dirt lay above their mother and little sister. Susan was taken aback when she noticed a solitary red rose atop her mother's tombstone. A card attached to it simply read, *"My Dearest Susie, I have never stopped loving you."* It was not signed. Jodi wondered who had left it there. Could it have been her father, Sean Johnson? *"Maybe,"* she thought, *"but unlikely."* He had in due course left the woman who had torn him from his wife and children. He naively believed that she would be faithful to him. But, she wasn't. After Susan died, he had freely expressed shame and remorse for leaving his family. But, Jodi knew that her father was not romantic or creative enough to have left the rose and the note.

It started to rain, steady and cool. Flashing a broad smile, Jodi visualized two angels, gleefully pouring out the rain from heaven.

As Jodi and Mike made their way through the cemetery, they slowly passed one headstone after another. Before they went through the iron gate at the exit, a hint of a rainbow began to enlighten the sky. And, Jodi whispered softly to her mother, *"Goodnight, my angel."*

Eager to see their own little children, they drove off into their new tomorrow where nothing would ever be the same. Jodi shed a tear as the country music blaring from the car radio caught her attention. *"It was so ironic that that particular song, her mother's favorite, would be playing right at that very moment,"* she thought.

She listened to the lyrics of Buddy Jewell's debut single, "Help Pour Out the Rain" (Lacey's Song):

Lord when I get to heaven, can I taste the milky way?
I don't want to come to visit cause I'm coming home to stay
and I can't wait to see my family and meet Jesus face to face
and do you think Lord
you could use just one more angel to help pour out the rain.

While Jodi was away from home, Mr. Bojangles parked his sizeable canine body on the ground in the main foyer of the Phan home. He lay strategically between the three bedrooms that cradled the tiny children. Sitting sentry, he slept with one eye open, scrutinizing every sound and motion.

Jodi had Mr. Bojangles since he was a pup. He was a Christmas present from her husband on their first holiday together. A integral part of their family, Mr. Bojangles had always been loyal, gentle and very affectionate and extremely protective of the three Phan babies. Everyone in the household loved him to pieces.

Due to Seng Phan's rigorous and inflexible schedule as a physician, his mother was recruited as a caretaker for the three children while Jodi was away. Noy Phan was a humble, modest woman in her early fifties. She was happy to help out, leaving her own husband to fend for himself for the duration of the trial. She was somewhat uncomfortable in the massive home that her son, the medical doctor and his family lived in. But, she was very eager to help out while her daughter-in-law was in New York City. She loved Jodi very much and she had had a friendly and mutually cherished relationship with Susan

Seng savored the delectable Loa cuisine that his mother dished up to him every evening. His favorites, all eaten with sticky rice, were laap a traditional chopped chicken dish; tam mak houng, a spicy salad made from sliced raw papaya, garlic, chili, peanuts, sugar, fermented fish sauce and lime juice; som moo, a fermented pork sausage; and his all time favorite, foe, a noodle soup, similar in style to the Chinese noodle soup found all over Asia. As much as Jodi tried to reconstruct the recipes, they never turned out like her mother-in-laws luscious creations.

In the early 1970s, as the Saigon regime in South Vietnam came to an end, Noy and her husband and their seven children left their homeland. They were classified as "boat people". In an exodus by sea, Noy and her family joined a steady stream of refugees.

In a rickety boat, floundering in the South China Sea, the Phan family, who had suffered great oppression, never gave up hope. They eventually established a brighter future in the United States. In an uphill struggle, with hard work and diligence they shaped a successful life. They lived in an unpretentious home and they had little in the way of material belongings. However, they had managed to educate all seven of their children at first-rate colleges and universities.

Noy was not the hugging, demonstrative grandmother that Susan was. She did not read to the children or play games with them. But, she loved them deeply and they in turn loved her. Jodi felt relief and gratitude that her mother-law- was available to assist her family during her absence. She was grateful for everything and everyone that she had in her life. Jodi knew quite well that her grandparents were in all probability rolling over in their graves at the mixture of races that befell their offspring. But, Jodi was so happy with her three beautiful children, a diversity of Asian and Caucasian, Catholicism and Buddhism. The world had changed! Racial prejudice was something that did not touch Jodi or her family.

When Michael left her off at her home, Jodi was overwhelmed with joy to be back with her family. Then, Michael was off to the airport on his way to his own family.

Chapter Forty-Two:

I Keep on Loving You

WEEKS LATER, AS THE RUGGEDNESS of winter become lighter and faded into the glorious renaissance of spring, Jodi hailed a cab from LaGuardia International Airport. She traveled by herself. She was dressed casually in a pair of boot cut jeans, a soft cotton pale yellow V-neck tee, and a navy blue mid length dress jacket. Her feet were comfy in a pair of penny loafers. She carried no suitcases. A Vera Bradley toggle tote was flung slackly over her shoulder. She didn't plan to be in the city very long. She had a return flight at midnight.

She thanked the yellow cab driver, handing him the fare with a generous tip. He smiled broadly, showing his gratitude. When she got out of the cab, her long legs felt a bit tipsy. Steadying herself, she drew her tote closer to her body. She was suppose to meet the woman at four o'clock. It was twenty minutes to four. Jodi picked the spot. They would meet at the 2nd Avenue Deli at 162 East 33rd Street between Lexington and 3rd Avenue.

The woman had been hesitant about meeting with her. Jodi couldn't criticize her for that. Jodi had to plead with her, calling her several times and the woman eventually caved in. This would be an awkward encounter for both of them. But, it was something that she had to do. Her brother and her uncle and her husband had each cautioned her about the meeting. But, she had to get together with the woman who had raised the evil person who had killed her mother. She had no idea what she and Juanita Moreno would say to each other. She had no idea whether this meeting would ease her sorrowful heart.

Her grandmother had passed away the week before. Her grandmother, who had raised three kind, gentle, honorable children, two of which had predeceased her, was lost to them for so many years, harboring the affects of dementia. When she was a little girl, Jodi remembered looking into her grandmother's vivid emerald eyes, smiling back at her with care and kindness. Deep within those eyes was the essence of a woman who had created an angel. She wanted to look deep within this woman's eyes and see the core of a woman who had created a monster.

A father may turn his back on his child; brothers and sisters may become inveterate enemies; husbands may desert their wives and wives their husbands. But a mother's love endures through all; in good repute, in bad repute, in the face of the world's condemnation, a mother still loves on, and still hopes that her child may turn from his evil ways, and repent; still she remembers the infant smiles that once filled her bosom with rapture, the merry laugh, the joyful shout of his childhood, the opening promise of his youth; and she can never be brought to think him all unworthy.

- Washington Irving

Jodi was very glad that she had made the trip to New York City. On her flight home from her meeting with Juanita Moreno, Jodi felt better, more relaxed and content. She realized that Jesus Moreno's mother was a decent person. Juanita knew that Jodi could never forgive Jesus for what he had done. That would be unimaginable. She did not intend to make excuses for him or defend him. She realized full well how horrible his deeds were. But, she did hope that she could help Jodi envision why he had become the man he was. As a child, he was torn between a caring and nurturing mother and a distant, immoral father. It would most likely have taken a team of psychologists many years to weed through the mess that produced the demons. Jesus's most important goal in life was to shelter the little girl under the tattered quilt. When it became apparent that he could no longer shield Manuela from the ills of the world, he lost his identity and transformed into a revengeful, vindictive man. He became the revenge seeker! Even before Manuela's problems arose, Juanita was convinced that he had done something so dreadful that it tormented him terribly. She had no idea what it was. But, it had left deep-rooted wounds. He was rotting in prison with no likelihood for parole. She visited him from time to time. But, he didn't encourage her.

Juanita would never forget her first visit with her son in prison. It was terribly upsetting for her. Her heart clenched tightly as the security guards hurriedly checked her identification, patted her down and walked her all the way through a narrow hallway. Finally, they came to a small room that was divided into eight isolation booths. Guided to a chair, she sat down at the first booth, facing a Plexiglas window, separated from the other windows by steel dividing walls. There was a large black woman in the booth next to her. The woman was chatting in street slang. Juanita could only make out bits and pieces of the conversation that the woman was having with the shadowy man at the other end of the window.

"The kids miss their daddy."

The woman pauses and smiles briefly.

"Daquan is kicking some ass in basketball. He's gonna be mad tall, just like you."

The woman stretches back in her chair and grins widely. She pushes a strand of jet black curls away from her face.

"Terrell and some kid from the south side had a fight and Terrell dogged him. The cops tried to grab 'im but he talked 'em out of it. He's got too much game for them."

Another pause. The woman seemed to be listening attentively.

"Rasheen is looking real fly these days. She's been rockin'. She's been hangin' with this dude from The Hill. He's gotta lot of scratch and he buys her cool threads."

The woman waves a finger into the air. She seems upset. Whatever the man has said to her seems to have touched a nerve. She begins to raise her voice a notch.

"Jamal has been talkin' shit about you again. Yo best kick his ass when you get out."

Now the woman is visibly irritated. She leans forward and talks straight into the window with the phone hanging loosely at her side.

"Now I gotta break it down for ya. I ain't mad atch ya or nothing' but I gotta say it straight up. I am shit outta paper. I need some bank."

The woman flares both hands into the air and stomps her feet like a kid in trouble.

Juanita could not hear any of the man's replies. But, she could tell by the woman's increased aggravation that his reactions were not what she anticipated.

The annoyed woman eventually slammed the receiver down, and huffed off in a bad mood to where a guard was stationed in a make-shift office. Her last words, before she faded into obscurity were,

"Go to hell, Marquis! You ain't all that! Know what I'm sayin'? You can march your fat ass right into hell!"

Ironically, the man was gone and Juanita and the guard were the only ones to hear her razor sharp remarks.

Cutting short Juanita's inquisitiveness about the other woman and the faceless companion, another gruff guard appeared and began drilling her on how to use the simple black phone that was perched on a narrow ledge in front of her.

"Pick it up, push the green button to talk. The yellow one to listen." he instructed sternly.

He left her there. She gawked at the blank window in front of her, for what seemed like several minutes. When Jesus finally emerged from somewhere behind the window, he looked in good physical shape. He had even put on a few pounds. She would always worry about him. He would always be her baby boy.

She smiled and he returned the gesture. Picking up the receiver to the phone and pushing the appropriate button, he let her talk first. *"Jesús, cada día, me preocupo por ti aquí. Tengo tanto miedo por ti,"* she told him sorrowfully.

He thanked her for coming and told her that it wasn't necessary for her to visit. He didn't really want her to see him there. He was doing fine. He told her not to worry. He was taking good care of himself and making the best of it all. He finally sat down and fidgeted for a few minutes with the phone on his end. He was nervous and so was she. He answered her questions.

"Yes, the food was pretty good and so far, he had made no enemies inside."

"No, he had not had any other visitors."

"No, the attorneys had not been in contact with him since the trial."

Lowering his eyes, his gaze met hers. It was in those eyes that she saw that the anger and that the hatred were still there. Fumbling with the buttons on the phone, she listened.

"Madre,"

His edginess eased a bit as he became more relaxed.

"You do not have to worry about money. There is plenty of that. I am putting everything in your name. After the restitution, there will plenty more for you. I do not want you to be hurting for money."

She covered her ears. She didn't want to hear about money. But, he persisted. Raising his voice to be understood, he was very direct.

"There are the cars. They are all worth a lot."

Jesus had acquired a 1966 apple red Corvette Milano, a gorgeous green 1988 Ferrari Testarossa with tan interior and his beloved 1988 Mercedes Benz 560 SL Roadster.

"And there's also the BMW G 650 Xcountry." That bike was Jesus's main ride. He had the time of his life when he rode the bike to Vegas. He loved the ecstasy of the spectacular scenery, as he twisted and turned on a mountainous journey that took him across canyons, cliffs and forests. Angelina was with him. Her sumptuous body, clad in leather, swayed to and fro, side to side in a steady tempo as she clutched her bosom closely to the hardness of his back.

He reminded his mother that he owned a substantial amount of property. There was an apartment building in el barrio with great rental potential and three lavish timeshares. One was located in beautiful Dorado, Puerto Rico, one was a fantastic Great Bay unit in Miami Beach and the other was a spectacular villa located one block off the Las Vegas Strip, between the MGM Grand and the Aladdin hotels.

There was an extravagant two- bedroom condo in one of West Soho's finest buildings. That is where he had Angelina salted away for the past several years. But, she was gone now. He had no idea where she was. He hadn't heard from her. But, his mother could easily sell the place for over five hundred thousand dollars.

There was the pawn shop, a dry cleaning business in East Harlem and a rare pistol collection that was worth over twenty-five thousand dollars. Juanita had no idea that her son had so many lucrative investments. Her stomach was tied in knots. She was tongue- tied. She didn't care a thing about all of the money. She didn't have the faintest idea about such things. She just sat there, not knowing how to respond.

Suddenly, with no warning, Jesus became rigid and with furrowed brow, he gazed angrily off into space for several minutes. Standing abruptly, he set the phone into its jacket and strolled off with the cocky gait of a gangster into his solitary, dreadful cell in that wretched place. Just like that. He was gone. No *"goodbyes."* No *"anything."* She walked away from the prison that day extremely troubled. She didn't feel like a woman with a lot of money. She felt like a woman with nothing at all.

Chapter Forty-Three:

Rising Every Time we Fall

SEVERAL WEEKS LATER, JODI RECEIVED a letter from Juanita Moreno. She opened it apprehensively. She had no idea what the woman could want to say to her. She read the letter fastidiously over and over a number of times. "Wow!" Jodi smiled freely. "Something worthwhile is really going to come from all of the suffering".

The apartment building that Jesus had once owned, was transferred to his mother. Juanita now held the title. It was a three story complex with twelve units that towered solidly built brownstones in the heart of Spanish Harlem. Juanita had decided to follow a lingering dream of hers and convert the first floor into a Puerto Rican Cultural and Performing Arts Center, which would focus on ethnic foods, music, festivals and entertainment, concentrating on Puerto Rican artisans, exhibits and musicians.

Her ultimate goal was enormous. She hoped to have the likes of Jennifer Lopez, Mark Anthony, Ricky Martin, Eva Longoria

Parker and other Latino celebrities arrive on the scene to shower the children with Puerto Rican pride. She would also provide shelter for women and children who were suffering from domestic violence. It would be a combination of ethnic delights and a safe haven for all.

She wanted Jodi's consent to call the center the *Manuela Moreno-Susan Johnson Center for Cultural and Performing Arts.* Jodi was honored, as she knew her mother would be. She gave Juanita her blessings and she and her brother and Uncle Benny all sent sizeable checks in support of the project.

Juanita's mission was to develop it into a world-class cultural complex, showcasing the best Latino artists of national and international acclaim.

The Performing Arts Center, with a bit of luck, would garner national attention in its serving as a model for its education initiatives in bringing the arts to a large urban community. On its Opening Night it became the fifth largest performing arts center in the U.S.

On a hot, heavy, hazy August evening in el barrio, many people gathered for the grand opening. The sizzling temperatures did not deter Susan's friends and family from attending. Jodi Phan and her husband and their children, Benny and Molly Deligrossi, Mike and Becky Johnson and their daughters, Matt and Ava Hastings, Jayne Marshall and Christina Grover all assembled together, seated at prominently positioned tables. Ellyn Carlson was there, along with other members of the OCFS staff.

Jimmy Dentes was there. He never did go to New England to live by the sea. He never did follow his dream of becoming a veterinarian. But, he did go to Cornell University and he earned a degree in Urban and Regional Studies, complimenting it with a law degree from Syracuse University.

He became a community organizer on the streets of New York City. He waged war against corrupt landlords, unfair politics, and racial injustice. He reached out to the homeless, the afflicted, the addicted, the elderly and the uneducated. He worked energetically to limit the over- representation of children of color and minority in the state detention centers.

Jimmy helped to launch city-wide centers offering safe, nurturing environments where kids could be kids, while discovering their purpose and God-given potential. These children learned to express themselves in fun and creative ways, while learning and testing valuable life skills. He offered them safe places to play, learn and grow.

Jimmy also had another aspiration and he worked very conscientiously to see it come to life. He was very vociferous and influential in facilitating the passage of a law prohibiting the writing, sending, or reading of text-based communication on a cell phone, while behind the wheel. He fulfilled a promise that he made to himself when he was at Walton. He was going to "make a difference."

Carlos Montego was there with his pretty wife and their two young sons. He was honored and flattered to be asked by Jaunita Moreno to give a formal address. It was August 15th. He was pleased to be celebrating his birthday at this most festive event. After his release from custodial confinement at Glasswing, the state established parens patriae power and Carlos went to live with a foster family in Western New York.

He graduated from high school in rural Allegany County and was able to attend Alfred University, where he graduated with honors in the criminal justice studies program. He later received a Master's degree in Institutional Management from Syracuse University's prominent Maxwell School. Ironically, years later, he returned to Glasswing. This time, he ran the show as the habilitation director.

He never forgot Susan and returned her kindnesses in his special relationship with hundreds of young men that he came in contact with every year. He came from where they came from. He understood their needs and he could identify with the pain in their lives. He helped young people achieve dignity and respect through knowledge, compassion, understanding, and love. Carlos recognized the need to arraign young offenders for their actions However, his main focus was rehabilitation and offering troubled young people the opportunity to lead happier, healthier, and more productive lives.

Jason Greene would have been there. But, he was in a nursing home in Staten Island. It was a sudden heart attack. His worn out heart failed him as swiftly as an assault from a Japanese sniper in World War II. He never saw it coming. After some risky and extensive surgery, he was convalescing, trying to get his spunk back. Looking regretfully at a forced retirement, Greene was already thinking of ways in which he could become a private investigator. His sense of humor still unbroken, he wrote to Jodi soon after he became ill, *"Old policemen never die, they just cop out."*

The gala grand opening was an elegant affair. Several very notable singers and musicians were on hand to overwhelm the crowds of guests and patrons with authentic Puerto Rican entertainment. The food was delicious and everyone had a wonderful time.

Carlos's speech was both inspiring and motivational. He started with:

"Good Evening. Today I am delighted to welcome you to the opening of this very extraordinary Performing Arts Center. It is a day for celebration and I am very pleased that you have all chosen to celebrate with us."

The remainder of the speech was uplifting, inspiring and motivational. His closing words were:

"In conclusion, let me remind you all gathered here tonight that when the fanfare and fuss fade away, after the champagne glasses are emptied and the speeches are over and done with, what we have here is something perpetual and momentous. Remembering the eloquent words of Langston Hughes,

"Hold fast to dreams, for if dreams die, life is a broken winged bird that cannot fly," Juanita Moreno held fast to her dream.

As he glanced in Jaunita's direction, she acknowledged him with a thumbs up.

"As for me, Confucius, had a saying that I have come to live by, "Our greatest glory is not in never falling but in rising every time we fall."

This time he looked intently at Jimmy. Without another word passing between them, they felt a common bond.

After a short pause and a clamorous thunder of applause, Carlos continued.

"Let's bow our heads for a moment of silence, remembering our own beloved Manuela and my dearly loved teacher, Susan.

Repeating it in Spanish, he bowed his own head.

"Vamos a bajar la cabeza por un momento de silencio, recordando nuestra propia nativo el barrio, Manuela y mi amado maestro, Susan."

When Juanita gave a final toast, Jodi had to fight back tears as a final surprise unfolded. In the front of the newly renovated building, amid lush grasses and an elaborate fountain, Juanita had planted a gorgeous Rose of Sharon tree. A brilliant blaze of red, the tree stood in front of a plaque with a commemorative inscription in English and in Spanish, that read;

> *A single rose can be my garden... a single friend,*
> *my world. ~Leo Buscaglia*
> *Two friends. Two lives, lost too soon.*
> *In loving memory of Manuela and Susan.*

> *Una sola rosa puede ser mi jardín ... un solo*
> *amigo, mi mundo. ~ Leo Buscaglia*
> *Dos amigos. Dos vidas, perdió demasiado pronto.*
> *En memoria de Manuela y Susan.*

Since the grand opening, the *Manuela Moreno- Susan Johnson Center for Cultural and Performing Arts* welcomed celebrated artists, ethnic icons, and some of the world's most treasured orchestral, dance, theater, and instrumental works, in addition to the best entertainers from Manhattan's dazzling collection of artists.

It also featured *El Centro Para Niños de Apreciación de la Música.* With the committed efforts of Jimmy Dentes' support, resources and collaboration, it offered the city children a space to feel valuable, to learn to express themselves through drama, dance, song and other forms of musical creativity. The kids loved to dance and sing, move and sway. It brought about a cultural extravaganza in el barrio.

The Center attracted over five hundred thousand patrons since its Opening Night. Most of the ticket buyers represented African-American, Hispanic/Latino-American, and Asian-American neighborhoods and school children from all walks of life.

Juanita Moreno fulfilled a dream to craft something worthy and meaningful in her community out of the catastrophic onset of heartbreak that came from the exclusive hand of her only son. Jodi Phan looked at the entire venture as a way for her mother's memory to be sealed and her mother's love for children to be emulated. Carlos Montego saw it as a way to move forward. Jimmy Dentes looked at it as penance and absolution. Following the ceremonies, as a gentle rain began to fall, Jimmy reflected in his native tongue, *"Alguien llamado Manuela estaba derramando la lluvia! Ella sabe que estoy aquí y ella forgies mí."*

Robert Clarence O'Neil, a multi-millionaire and prominent businessman became one of the center's nameless benefactors. Until the day he died at the age of ninety two, he sent out anonymous checks to support the project. He also showered the center with red roses every August 2nd. Juanita Moreno marveled at the gesture, wondering, *"Who exactly was he?" "Why his interest in the center?" "What was the significance of the red roses? "Why on August 2nd every year?"*

After O'Neil's death, his only surviving relative, a niece, found a note attached to a discolored Polaroid snapshot of a pretty young girl. The note and photo were slipped between some business cards in O'Neil's wallet. The girl in the photo was a pony-tailed teen, clothed in tie dyed shorts and a sleeveless, white islet blouse who wore large sunglasses. She was sitting in front of a frothy waterfalls. Glowing and beaming, her smile seemed to light up the portrait.

Behind the girl, a road sign could be distinguished quite easily. It showed dark yellow lettering, outlined in black beneath an arrow pointing in the direction of the falls. The lettering said, *"Larch Meadows."* The niece vaguely remembered the spot from her days at Cornell. It was a wetland area near Buttermilk Falls. She had hiked the nature trail that encircled Larch Meadows one or two times. The attractive young girl in the photo appeared to be about fifteen or sixteen years old. She clutched a single red rose close to her heart. The attached note simply read:

August 2nd, 1965

High up.
Above the clouds.
Far beyond my reach.
Susan and I will meet again.
Our time together on this Earth was short lived,
For us, our time is yet to come. And, it will!

R.O.N

The niece, realizing that the note and photo must have been important to her uncle, tenderly tucked them into the classic white marble urn that held his cremated ashes. And, hence, the love story of Susan and Robby never ceases, but goes on full circle... for time without end.

The Ending

The Insanity is Over!

WHEN HE STROLLED OUT OF the Griffin State Penitentiary in the Catskills, he shielded his eyes from the bright glow of the crimson sky. Nearly blinded by its brightness, he put both of his hands over his eyes. He had spent the last thirty years of his life in Cell Block D. He entered there as a young man, broad-shouldered and robust. He was leaving there with high blood pressure, gout, a stomach paunch and a receding hairline.

He didn't look at all like the fine-looking man that he was at one time. The hair that he had left was a dull, lifeless gray color. His shoulders were stooped and the old bounce in his pace was now replaced with a slow and monotonous way of walking. He wore a short well- groomed gray beard close to his face. He was dressed in clothing that was a modest gift from the state of New York. He was sent forth into the world with two hundred and fifty dollars to retrigger his new life.

All of his family was gone. There was no one left to go home to see. Not that there was any one who ever really cared any way. He had his instructions. He knew exactly what to do. He had only one choice. The course of action was simple. He would travel by bus to the city, take a yellow cab to Sammy Ngyuan's laundry, get the envelope and proceed from there.

Walking into the musty smelling laundry, he saw Sammy sitting behind the same disorganized clutter that he sat behind years before. Sammy looked as if he was frozen in time, except that he looked older, thinner and worn-down. The years had taken their toll on him. Time did him no favors.

He asked Sammy for the envelope and the old Cambodian shuffled through some boxes on a shelf before he found the small brown envelope that had been hidden there for over a quarter of a century. Handing over the envelope, Sammy's toothless grin was proverbial. The cavernous wrinkles on his forehead overwhelmed his ripened features.

The ex con left the laundry. He hastily tore into the paper. Holding the key tightly in his hand, he considered his next move. A short walk to the train station led him to a wall of safe deposit boxes. He scanned them carefully, finding the one that the key would fit. It was number "eighty six." His hand shook a bit as he opened the small square medal door and took out its contents, one hundred, thousand dollar bills.

The next day, he found himself on a plane. He left from JFK and was embarking on the only future there was for him. The flight was uneventful until the plane approached the majestic, awe-inspiring Washington Cascades. The lengthily range of forested mountains presented a breathtaking view.

He took a Sea-Tac shuttle into the heart of the city of Seattle and then a short cab ride into a charming water front community, a stone's throw from the panoramic vistas of Puget Sound. He found himself wanting to explore the beckoning waterfront. But, he had no time to waste. He asked the cabdriver to stop when they came upon some upscale bistros, clusters of stylish shops, decorative cafes, trendy boutiques, and a number of posh salons. He gave the driver a wholesome tip and began walking along the metro district onto tree lined avenues.

He stopped at a chic florist shop and bought a colossal bouquet of long stemmed red roses, gift wrapped stylishly in red tissue paper. *"My prop,"* he mused.

He had memorized the address. He found his destination without difficulty. The home was located in an expansive lakefront residential community. It was charming and very welcoming. She lived well in a sprawling, red brick ranch with a flourishing landscape, which was enhanced by a pretty white picket fence. The front door was polished in a rich emerald color.

"This house fits her to a tee," he smiled to himself. *"Very voguish, fashionable. Just like she was."*

He walked the elegant entrance way towards the alluring front portico. He climbed a few steps and tapped softly at the door. Within a few moments, she opened it.

Looking upon her face for the first time in many years, he was startled for a second. Time had been good to her. She aged with poise, gracefully. She was as stunning and dazzling as she had always been. Her gorgeous ruby tresses were shoulder length, in a cascade of curls. Her brilliant blue eyes were still radiant. Her body had been well preserved. She looked fit and healthy, firm and sexy. She did not recognize him. She smiled at him and gasped slightly when she saw the gaily wrapped bouquet.

"For me?" she chuckled.

"Only if you are Emily," he answered teasingly.

"Who are they from, I wonder," she giggled. Knowing full well they had to be from Ryan. Her husband would often surprise her with flowers, delivered to her at the door from exclusive floral shops.

After handing her the bouquet, he asked her if it would be too much of an inconvenience for a weary delivery man to use her bathroom. She hesitated only briefly. She appreciated the delivery men who hand delivered the flowers. *"This one was older than usual,"* she thought.

"Of course," she smiled eagerly. *"Please do. We have a small powder room right here in the mud room area. You have quite a jaunt back to the florist shop. Help yourself."*

Four hours later, her husband discovered her lifeless body, laying on the mud room floor. She was so still.

"How could that be," he mourned. *"Emily was never still. She was a bubble ready to explode! She was a firecracker! A beautiful burst of energy!"*

The Seattle police considered it to be a burglary. It was most likely a kid looking for drug money. Her wallet was gone, along with some jewelry, including her diamond rings. The only other thing missing, they discovered, was a quart of Crown Royal in its blue velvet bag.

This sort of thing didn't happen in their world. Ryan was shaken with anguish and his three daughters were enduring enormous pain.

Three weeks later, Chico sat on a stool at *The Southern Palms Tiki Bar* on a long and beautiful stretch of beach. He landed in one of Puerto Vallarta finest five star resorts, surrounded by golden beaches and magnificent sunsets. He was sipping on a mojito, eyeing bikini clad beauties amid an oasis of palms.

The blistering sun kissed his cheeks. The exquisiteness of the resonance of the ocean waves bathed his soul with ecstasy. The sweet nectar of the mojito saturated his taste buds. The pretty women before him fulfilled his visual desires.

Jesus grimaced. His crazed mind was spiraling in a fit of fury when he received the message from Chico.

"Mission accomplished, Jesus. The insanity is over! La locura se acabó!"

Another Book By Diane Pellicciotti Kone

Goodnight, My Angel

Excerpt from the Lansing Star Online Newspaper

By Dan Veaner, November 25, 2005

"Goodnight My Angel" is a story about love and endurance, and great personal tragedy. Set in 1950s Cortland, it tells about Italian/American Susan Deligrossi, who falls in love with an Irish boy that she is not allowed to marry. So they go their separate ways and each marry other people. Later she has a daughter who is born with a congenital heart defect. Facing challenge after challenge Susan struggles to piece together her life.

If this sounds like the makings of a Romance novel, that is exactly what it is. Lansing author Diane Pellicciotti Kone based it on a key event in her life, when her own daughter, Paula Daniels, died at age 12 in 1994 of a congenital heart defect. Ms. Kone, at that time Diane Daniels, was a Lansing teacher who taught in the Elementary and Middle Schools for 33 years.

When her daughter died, Ms. Kone wrote as a way of consoling herself. "I cloistered myself in a fishing cottage on the St. Lawrence River and I wrote a book about the tragedies and the treasures of Paula's life. It took four summers. I ended up in a cottage on Little York Lake, which was closer. I needed to be near the water."

"When Paula was really sick she begged me to take her to Florida." With the doctor's encouragement she made the trip and Paula got to see the ocean. "I guess that's what drew me to the water," says Ms. Kone.

Her husband Dave Kone and surviving daughter Amy wanted her to publish the book, but she felt she would have to rewrite it as fiction in order to share it with others. " I couldn't let it go. I couldn't send this book out for people to read and buy." So she began rewriting the book as fiction about a year ago, and it was just published recently.

She drew from her experiences growing up in the Italian neighborhood in Cortland. Susan, her main character, is not allowed to marry the boy she loves, in a Romeo and Juliet style story. She goes through many challenges in her life, including having a child with a congenital heart defect. "Most of the story isn't me," Ms. Kone explains. "That part of it is. It's sad, but it's uplifting in the sense that Susan is able to pick up the pieces and move on. The ending is kind of a twist."

"A lot of it is about growing up in Cortland and growing up in the Italian neighborhood in the ethnic area where the railroad tracks really did separate. You had the blue collar workers on one side and the more affluent ones on the other. My grandfathers worked on the railroad. Since they were Italians who couldn't speak the language they were given the more dangerous, dirty jobs. The Irish, who were also immigrants from the same time period could speak the language, therefore they had the better jobs."

Ms. Kone enjoyed novel writing. "I tended to work better in the middle of the night. Dave would bring me cups of coffee and I would type away. It's great to write, because you have all of this control. You name the characters, you put them in settings that you want. It's very empowering."

LaVergne, TN USA
31 January 2010
171619LV00007B/68/P